HERE WITH ME

HEIDI MCLAUGHLIN

here
with me

HEIDI MCLAUGHLIN

Praise for Here With Me

Oh God, Here With Me had my heart racing and my eyes burning. Filled with angst, passion and conspiracy and laced with traces of young love, Heidi McLaughlin's latest is a one-sitting must-read.

Delving deep into the intricately woven pasts of twins and current Navy SEALS, Evan and Nate Archer, and one fiery redhead, Ryley, Here With Me not only holds the reader captive with the threesome's past and present relationships, but also spins a scandalous web—The Navy has duped someone and it is unclear who started the never-ending lies.

Over the last six years, Evan Archer was declared dead while his brother slipped into his life, taking his own twin's place in the heart of his woman and their child. Now Evan is back and Nate is gone, and no one knows who is lying or telling the truth, and as readers, we are left with raw emotion and gut-wrenching feelings while the story unravels in front of us.

McLaughlin's voice is authentic, raw and genuine while bringing this story of love for both a single woman and an entire country to life... *Rachel Blaufeld, author of Electrified and Smoldered*

Simply breathtaking! Evan and Ryley had me mesmerized, rooting for them to find their way through unimaginable love and devastation. I sobbed, I laughed along with them, and at times, I wanted to throw this book across the room! HERE WITH ME is a story I won't soon forget, and I'm desperate for more... *Rachel Harris, author of The Fine Art of Pretending*

This book is hands down Heidi's best yet. Coupled with her ability to weave an intricate tale such as this with loveable and relatable characters such as Evan and Ryley sets this book apart from the rest. Heidi holds your attention with lies, mystery and a timeless love story that will grip your heart and leave you begging for more. Evan will melt your heart and Ryley's plight will pull it apart. This is a book you don't want to miss. The roller coaster of emotions is worth the ride!... *Jennifer Wolfel, Wolfel's World of Books*

To all the men and woman who serve our country, who protect our country, I appreciate you.

No happy homecoming for SEALs declared dead by Navy By Art Liberty

SAN DIEGO – We have all seen and read about the happy homecomings of military members returning from deployment. Tearful but smiling family members embrace uniformed moms, dads, sons and daughters and welcome them back into their loving arms. High-ranking military and political officials give speeches lauding the bravery of the returning men and women. Sometimes there is even a band playing cheerful and patriotic music.

That is the joyful scene that we have become used to seeing on the internet, television, social media and newspapers. But that was not the welcome home reportedly experienced by four members of Navy SEAL Team Three, based in Coronado, CA.

They deplaned after a long flight from their theater of operations to be met by – no one. Instructed to take taxis from the airfield, the SEALs made their own way home to families that were anything but overjoyed to see them. The reason? All four were dead, according to the Navy. Funerals had been held with full military honors. "Taps" was played, a rifle salute was performed, and in a meaningful ritual peculiar to the Navy's elite warrior SEALs, fellow SEAL team members removed their Trident insignias and embedded them into the lids of the caskets in a poignant and symbolic goodbye to fallen brothers-in-arms.

Sources close to the four men report that the SEALs, deployed for an unheard of six years, were regularly provided with "care packages" purportedly from their families at home, including items such as newsy letters and family photographs. The men are reportedly devastated by the thought that their loved ones believed them to be dead and buried for the past several years.

Lcdr. Becca Dawn, spokesperson for the Naval Special Warfare Command in Coronado, the command with authority over all Naval Special Warfare forces, said four days ago, "I am not aware of this issue or these men. I will have to get back to you." So far there has been no further comment and Lcdr. Dawn has not returned numerous messages. Several attempts were made to contact the Public Affairs Officer of Naval Special Warfare Group One, the parent command immediately over SEAL Team Three, have also not been returned. Former Navy Lt. Candy Brotz, past spokesperson for the command and now a reporter for Military News noted, "It is unheard of for SEALs to be deployed for that length of time. The circumstances are not only unusual, they are highly suspicious. The Navy doesn't just tell families that their sailor is dead without a lot of documentation and investigation."

Clearly this incident calls for answers from Navy authorities. Meanwhile, four traumatized families and four brave warriors try to rebuild shattered lives, if that is even possible.

ONE

Ryley

EACH STEP I TAKE IS PAINFUL. Not in the sense that I've been physically injured — unless you can count my heart being torn out and ripped to shreds, twice, as being physically hurt — but in the sense that my body aches with any type of movement. I'm sore all over from too much crying and a lack of eating. Withering away to nothing, as my best friend, Lois has been saying for the past two weeks.

The fact that it's been two weeks since my life has been turned upside down flipped inside out and run through the ringer stops me mid-step. Lois smashes into my back, no doubt looking at her phone, texting someone she shouldn't be and meddling in my affairs. Even though I love her, I want her to stop. I want to wake up from this nightmare and have my life go back to the way it was six years ago.

Lois places her hand on my back, urging me silently to take the next step, and the next one and the next one after that. She's been my rock for as long as I can remember, and surprisingly there was a time when I didn't need her as much, but that's all changed.

At the top of the staircase sits a table with a small bouquet of freshly picked flowers, a nice touch to the drab location.

When Lois pulled in front of the building, I recoiled in my seat. The brick building, old and worn with age, shows no sign of being welcoming. The sidewalk is cracked and weeds grow in between the slabs. The only saving grace is the park across the street, and while it's empty, it looks inviting, if not a place to escape.

Lois opens the door before I can raise my hand to knock. She's impatient with me and I understand why. I know deep down she's afraid I'm going to turn and run. Believe me the thought has crossed my mind a time or two. I know it's not the answer, but it makes the most sense. If I can't be found, I can't be hurt, and I've had far too much hurt in my life to last me until my last breath. With her hand on my back, she gives me a gentle nudge to step into the office. The woman behind the glass wall looks up briefly and gives us a half smile. She probably feels the same way I do about the building. It's lacking in life, much like I am right now.

After giving her my name, I sit down next to Lois. Her face is now stuffed in a magazine, and she's ignoring me. This is her idea of tough love. I've been down this path with her before so I know what to expect. You'd think by now I'd be a pro and can deal with whatever is thrown my way, but I'm not. It seems that every few years my idea of happiness turns into a weak excuse for life.

My name is called, and I'm directed through an open door. The room I step into is lackluster and cold. I cross my arms to ward off an impending shiver and chastise Lois for making me wear a dress today. My cardigan is resting in the backseat of her car when it should be on my shoulders.

"Good morning. What's your name?"

It's in the chart on your desk, I want to yell out, but refrain. Lois would likely hear me and scold me like a child. I'd take it though because she'd be right. The lady behind the desk doesn't ask me to sit down or guide me to the chair or couch in her office. She doesn't even look at me. This meeting is feeling a bit too impersonal for my taste, and as I reach for the door, I hear her clear her throat.

"Ryley, I like to ask my patients to say their names so that their identities aren't forgotten when we start discussing why you're here."

It makes sense, I think. I opt to sit on the couch, but only on the edge. I don't want to be comfortable or complacent.

"Ryley Clarke," I answer, letting my name flow easily from my lips.

"Tell me, Ryley, what brings you in today?"

Of course she wastes no time punching me in the gut. If it weren't figuratively, I'd flinch and let her know that it's not okay to hit, but instead I straighten my back and ponder the question that seems to have brought me to this point in my life. A point where I'm required, no begged, to enter therapy to help figure out the rest of my life. Maybe not even the rest, but the next step. Either step I take leads me down a path of love, pain and irreparable hurt.

Most importantly, I don't want to be here. I don't think talking to a third party with a psyche degree is the answer. Sadly, I'm the only one who feels that way. I've been told therapy will help, but I'm not so sure it will. You can't fix something that has been destroyed for years. We aren't a family of teddy bears with missing eyes or ears that can be sewn back on making us look somewhat new. We're a damaged bunch, destined for nothing but heartache.

I pick at the threadbare couch that I chose to sit on. It looked more comfortable than the chair in front of her. It's royal blue, or at least it used to be. I think at one time it was probably soft, plush and very comfortable, and people didn't have a problem lying back, closing their eyes and letting all their worries flow from their mouths. You would think that with the many people that come through the door, a new couch could be purchased. I may be wrong in my assumption. I likely am. This couch holds secrets that no one ever wants out, and it's about to know mine too. Maybe that's why she keeps it this way.

"Why am I here today?" the words are a whisper on my lips. I can barely hear them myself and know she can't hear me. Clearing my throat, I keep my eyes downcast and away from her face. The last thing I want is for her to see the pain in my eyes. That's for me and me alone when I stare in the mirror, asking myself how and why.

"I'm here so you can fix… this." The words are bitter and angry. I spread my arms out wide, and my knuckles scrape the side of the worn out armrest. I pull my right hand to me, examining my fingers for any signs of damage. A sliver maybe, something to cause pain, anything to make me feel. I have nothing.

I lean forward, determined not to cry. I don't know why I'm here. I healed. I moved on. We moved on. Life was good, not better, but manageable. We were happy. We laughed and loved and we missed him terribly, but we woke up each day determined to make a new happy memory. But then life — no, I take that back — the military made that all change.

If I were a conspiracy theorist, I'd say this was all planned, but honestly, what do they care about my life? Nothing, that's for damn sure. They don't care that they've ruined the last six years of my life because of some clerical error. "Sorry," is all they could be bothered to say.

They're sorry.

I realize now that I've spoken, the floodgates are open, and I can't get my words out fast enough. She, the one who sits behind a desk taking notes, doesn't have a clue as to what I've been through, but I'm about to tell her.

"I don't know why I'm here. I'm not sure a session or a million sessions can fix my life right now. People have told me that time heals all wounds, but they're full of shit. I think when that saying was coined, they meant a scratch or a bump, not a hole in the middle of your chest that you'd have to put back together piece by piece. A hole so big that when you breathe in, it burns and makes you ache all over. One that makes you beg for someone to show you mercy, even if no one will because they all feel the same way as you. And was I ever really healed, or did I wake-up one morning and decide that I needed to move on?"

"It does take time to heal, Ryley, and everyone has to do it at their own pace."

I laugh out loud and adjust the way I'm sitting. I wish I hadn't worn a dress today, but Lois insisted, and I'm at a point in my life where I just do as she says, so I put on a yellow sundress and pulled my hair into a blue ribbon. That's as good as it gets for me right now. But sitting here, I want to be in sweats. I want my white socks covering my bare toes, and I want to be buried under an oversized sweatshirt. I want to hide.

"Time is my enemy. Time is the one thing I don't have and can't afford to lose. Time…" I shake my head and look toward the window. I bite my lip and close my eyes. My mind is blank. I refuse to see their images. I don't want to look, or remember. "I need to find a way to stop time or reverse it." I nod. "Reversing time would be ideal. If I could do that, I wouldn't be sitting here right now. My life… it'd be on the path that I created, that I worked hard for, but it's not. I'm standing in the center of the Interstate with traffic coming at me from both directions waiting… desperately waiting for someone or something to change everything that has happened in the last six years. So no, time doesn't heal anything. It just prolongs the hurt and pain.

"It sounds like you've had a lot to deal with, maybe more than others. Do you find solace in your friends?"

I shake my head. "I have two very close friends. One is from high school, she and her husband moved down here once the twins where stationed here. The other is a military wife. Any other friends I had bailed. I'm sure they didn't bail because of me, but because of the military. You move on, ya know? They don't want to associate…" I stop and think about that word. "Associate isn't the correct word; it's fear. They see what I went through and fear rips through their bodies, and they do what their bodies tell them: fight or flight. They all chose flight because they're all afraid they'll go through the same thing one day."

"What else do you experience from your friends and family?"

Easy question. "Pity. I got so sick and tired of the hugs and the pats on the shoulder. The looks — those were never-ending. I didn't need to see the pity in their eyes as they went from looking at me to looking at my belly. Everyone is sorry, but what exactly are they sorry for? Are they sorry that they voted for the people who sent our military to war? Are they sorry that their children aren't out defending our country? What are they sorry for?" My voice rises with my last question. I want to know. What goes through someone's mind when they tell you they're sorry that your loved one has died?

"I always want to ask why. Why are you sorry? Did you do something that I'm not aware of? Did you pull the trigger or supply the enemy with equipment to do harm? No, I didn't think so. Thing is, all the pity looks are back and each one brings me to my knees because guess what? They're all sorry again, and this time it's not going to matter what decision I make. Someone will be hurt. For that, they can be sorry."

"Ryley, I'm going to ask you again why are you here today?"

For the first time since I walked in the door, I look at the therapist. Her hair is cut short, framing her face. It's brown, but muted. There's no vibrancy to her color. It's dull and outdated, much like her couch. Her white, long-sleeved shirt is buttoned high, as if it wants to choke the life out of her. Her cat-like glasses perch on the edge of her nose, and she reclines in her chair with her pad of paper resting on her lap, her pen poised to write down my words at a moment's notice.

"I'm here because six years ago I lost the love of my life, but now he's back from the dead, and in a few weeks I'm set to marry my best friend. His brother."

TWO

Evan

I'M IN A PLACE I never thought I'd be: a civilian therapist's office, sitting in civilian clothing. Give me a uniform and I'm comfortable, but the lack of dress blues staring at me from behind the desk has my nerves on edge. There will be questions that she's going to ask that I'll refuse to answer because I took an oath, and I'll stand by that oath until I'm six feet under. I know she's just doing her job, but I protect mine. She'll want answers that I don't have. If I had them, I wouldn't be sitting here.

My back is stiff against the wooden chair. Most of the padding that existed when this office opened is missing, leaving the back of the chair uncomfortable. It could be from the constant grinding one does while being scrutinized, or from the slouching that our bodies do when we naturally become despondent or bored. There's a pre-determined dent, which indicates where my back should fit in nicely, only mine doesn't. It's pressed as tight as it can be, looking for the smallest bit of comfort. Surprisingly, I'm given none. I've been living with pain for the past five or six years – I've lost count – and don't see the pain subsiding in the foreseeable future.

"Welcome, why don't you start my telling me your name?"

"Chief Petty Officer Archer."

"Is that your first name, Archer?" she asks. "I like to be personal and go on a first-name basis with my patients."

"No, my first name is Evan."

"How are you today, Evan?"

My fingers itch from sitting still. I don't want to be here, but the alternative is less appealing. Part of me is running back to base and to the security it provides from the outside world, but the other part of me, the part I'm listening to, is hoping that when I'm done here everything I thought I had will be mine again. If not, I don't know what I'm going to do. Everything I knew I had, everything that I thought was waiting for me, isn't. That's a hard pill to swallow knowing you're coming home to a family, but they don't want you there.

"Today, I'm okay." I clear my throat and cross my leg over my knee. It's ninety degrees outside and common sense would say to wear shorts, but I couldn't bring myself to think I'd be that relaxed here today. My black slacks are creased and lint free. My black socks are the same shade as my pants, and my shoes are polished enough to see my reflection. I pull at my pant leg and place my hand on my ankle to hold my leg in place. I have to put my hands somewhere. I have to keep them occupied because visions of strangling someone cloud my mind if I don't keep them busy.

The therapist picks up her glasses and places them on her face. I watch as her hand slides them up the bridge of her nose until they're resting where she needs them, only for them to slowly start to slide back down. She doesn't stop what she's doing to push them back into place. She continues to write as her hand flies across her yellow notepad in a hurried fashion.

"Do you know why you're here, Evan?"

My hand leaves my ankle as the hem of my slacks becomes the most fascinating piece of clothing I own. I pull, push and straighten the cuff repeatedly. Of course I know why I'm here, but I don't think she can fix my issues and if she can, I have doubts that the fix will work.

"Yes."

"Are you here of your own accord."

No, I'm not, I want to say but don't. My sock needs adjusting, so that's what I do now. Again with the pull, push and straightening. Again, I avoid eye contact.

"Yes, I am," I lie. As much as I don't want to be here and would prefer to do this on base with people I trust... trusted I'm here because this is what Lois says needs to happen. She says Ryley needs this, and I know she was here earlier today. Other than that, I have no idea what happened. I haven't seen her for a week, again per Lois' instructions and not since I showed up on our... her front porch with my bag sitting at my feet and my hat cuffed under my arm.

"How would you like to start?"

I shrug, not knowing how these types of meetings are supposed to go. I was just told to show up, to be here on time and to try. So far I've accomplished two of the three, but I'm not sure how I'm going to try when I have no idea how everything became so messed up to begin with.

"Would you like to talk about Ryley?"

I shrug again. I want to talk to Ryley, period, but she won't return my phone calls. "She's my favorite subject," I say before I know the words are coming out of my mouth.

The therapist takes off her glasses and sets them down on her desk before folding her hands. I glance at her briefly and see that she's smiling gently at me. I hope that's a good sign, that it means everything with Ryley went smoothly. I hate that she was here earlier, and I couldn't be. I wanted us to do this together but was advised against it. My life is all about advisement these days. Everyone and their grandmother has advice for me. Everyone knows what's best, but none of them know shit.

Six years ago, I left home on a mission. I was told it'd be easy, in and out. There was nothing easy about what we were doing and why it took so long. Communication breakdowns, wrong Intel. It didn't matter because once we were airborne we were targets, and nothing was going to save us.

She clears her throat getting me to look at her again. I know she's waiting for me to elaborate, but I can't. Talking about Ryley hurts me physically. I've missed her so much over the years that when I imagined our homecoming, it was something out of those ridiculous fairytale romances she was always telling me about. My mind pictured her dropping whatever was in her hands, as they would cover her mouth in shock. Her eyes would fill with unshed tears and she'd run to me, leaping into my arms. I'd spin her around a few times before setting her back on the ground where I'd cup her face in my hands and kiss her until we could no longer breathe.

That didn't happen, except for the shocked face and tears. My reunion was nothing like you read about or see on television, the exact opposite, actually. I didn't see happiness in her face; I saw anger and hurt. I had hurt her and didn't know how. The only way to fix it sits in front of me, waiting for me to answer all her questions.

"Why are you here today, Evan?"

I drop my leg and rub the spot where my ankle was resting. I adjust myself in the uncomfortable chair and clear my throat as my hands rub down my legs, wiping away the sweat on my palms.

"Six years ago, the love of my life told me we were having a baby. I asked her to marry me and left a few days later on what was supposed to be an easy mission. Each mission is different. We know this going in, but this is our job. It's what we do, and we do it proudly. I was told that I'd be home for the birth of the baby. They'd make sure of it. From prior experience, I knew they'd keep their word."

Except someone didn't.

"You've been gone a long time, Evan."

I lean forward to relieve some of the ache in my back. "We never know how long we're going to be gone. Ideally, you get in, get the job done and get out. It was only supposed to be for a few months. I was trying to keep track of Ryley's due date and when it got close, my R & R was nowhere to be seen. My commander said it was coming and before I knew it, those months turned into a year and that year turned into six. Every time I'd check in, I was told they were working on an immediate extraction of just me so I could get home to meet my son, but it never came. They assured me that my brother knew everything."

"But he didn't?"

I sit back harder than I intend to and my muscles flinch. I shake my head. "I don't know. I don't know who to trust. The men that promised to protect me say yes, but the man who shares my DNA, who was supposed to protect what's mine, is on his own mission and I can't ask him. I can't confront him and demand that he tell me everything."

"Do you think the Navy could be wrong?"

"I don't know what to think. I went to do my job and when I came home expecting my family to be waiting for me, I was met with my fiancée wearing another man's ring, a ring that belongs to my twin brother."

"I'm going to ask you again, Evan, why are you here?"

This time I don't hesitate. "I want to know how I get my girl back. I miss Ryley like crazy, and I want to know my son."

THREE

Ryley

___

THE THERAPIST STANDS AND walks over to her water dispenser. My eyes are trained on her every movement and I don't know why. Do I find her fascinating, or is my mind looking for an escape route? Unfortunately for me, on the other side of the door is a brick wall known as Lois Parker, waiting to stop me.

"You can't run," Lois reminded me last night. She stood in front of my door, blocking my exit. We were both crying, our tears meaning something different. My bags were packed and waiting by the door. I was going to leave. That was my answer – to be far away from the place that caused me nothing but pain. It didn't matter that I have no place to go, or that I'd be ripping my son away from his family. In my mind, running is the easiest answer.

She walks over to me with a glass of water, holding out her hand but keeping her distance. I suppose this is how a therapist stays detached though, isn't it? I couldn't do a job like this. I'd become emotionally invested with each person. I'd want to hold and coddle them and tell them that yes, everything will be okay, but it never is. Yes, I'd be a liar.

"How did you meet Evan?" she asks after taking a drink from her glass before sitting back down in her chair.

I can't help but smile. It was a moment that changed my life. "I was sixteen and had just moved to Bremerton, Washington. My mom, she's a Navy JAG lawyer, and she had a transfer to the Navy base there. The movers were unloading our truck, and I was in the way, so my dad told me to explore. This was the first time we weren't going to live on base, so I was a little hesitant to just walk around, but I did as my dad suggested. I don't think I was two blocks away from my house when I was pegged in the head by a football."

"A football?" the therapist clarifies.

I nod. "I was walking by a park. It was busy. There were kids swinging and people playing in the pool. I had stopped to look. I was going to go home and ask my dad if I could go swimming, but just as I turned, bam! I was tossed back onto my butt. A boy came running over – he didn't even look for cars when he crossed the street. He kneeled down in front of me, and his eyes – God they were so full of life – they examined me. He pulled my hand away from my head without saying a word. I knew he felt bad. His shoulders slumped forward, and he started rubbing the back of his neck. His friends were yelling at him to throw the ball back. They were more concerned with finishing their game. They didn't care that I was dying." He stood, and I thought "'*Ryley, say something you idiot. Here's your chance to finally speak to a hottie,*'" but my mouth just moved up and down like I was a goldfish begging for water. He threw the ball back but didn't leave. He kneeled down in front of me again and said, "'*Shit, babe, I've gone and messed up your pretty face.*'" I was so taken because he called me pretty that I didn't care what I looked like at that moment.

"He helped me to my feet and didn't let go of my hand. I can still see us standing there, on the sidewalk in early September hand in hand, Evan looking down at me. It was a picture-perfect moment that I wish I could go back and capture. I think that's the day I fell in love with Evan Archer even though I didn't know him.

"He was the first boy to seriously hold my hand. His fingers slid in between mine and he squeezed them just enough to send chills up my arm. My heart was beating so fast I thought for sure I was going to have a heart attack right there on the sidewalk. He tugged me toward him and cocked his head to the side. It was his way of asking me to come with him and at that point, I'd follow him anywhere he'd ask. Evan walked us across the street and back to the football game. I knew my palm was sweating but there was no way I was letting go of his hand. This moment was all my favorite romance stories coming to life. I was one of the characters off the pages experiencing love at first sight and there was no way I was going to turn away.

"When he looked at me and said, "'*Everyone, this is…*'" I thought 'wow' my own Prince Charming. I don't know if he didn't finish his sentence because he didn't know my name or if it was because of the way I was staring at him while he smiled at me. And not just any smile, but the kind that makes your knees weak. The one that makes you forget that you're an educated human being, and even though your mind is yelling at you to scream out your name, you can't because you don't remember it. You can't because you're lost in the ocean-blue eyes of the guy holding your hand."

My jaw starts to lock up, the sure sign that tears are on the way. These are happy memories but swallowed up by sad tears. I bring my glass to my lips and drink in an attempt to ward off the impending outbursts. The glass is half empty when I'm done. I'm not a half full type of gal anymore. I take a deep breath and continue.

"'*What's your name, babe?*'" He called me babe from the moment he met me. I had never had a nickname before other than Ry, and I didn't care what he called me as long as he kept talking. By the gleam in his eyes, he knew that he could call me whatever he wanted, and I'd be okay with it. He also knew, without a doubt, that I was his.

"'*Ryley Clarke*,'" I told him proudly and with a smile. He never took his eyes off of me to repeat my name either. It was like we were destined to meet even if it meant him causing me bodily harm.

"'*Ryley, I like that name. I'm Evan Archer. These are my friends.*'" He pointed to a group of guys all about the same age as Evan. Even though half were shirtless, dirty with grass stains and mud, I could only focus on them briefly before turning my gaze back to Evan. He had my sixteen-year-old self-mesmerized just by calling me babe and at that moment, it was enough for me.

"He spread his sweatshirt out on the ground and offered me a place to sit. He asked me to stay and watch the game because he wanted to talk to me some more, but needed to finish playing. I sat there with my legs pulled to my chest, fascinated. It didn't matter – at least not to me – that I was supposed to be exploring. I was content, happy.

"I watched as he ran down the makeshift football field and scored. He had a touchdown dance that made me laugh. After each one, he'd run by me and wink. I didn't know what I was getting into that day, but I still wouldn't trade it for anything.

"When he was done playing he sat down beside me, and we waited for his friends to leave, and all but one left. "'*This is my brother, Nate.*'" There were two of them, each one as cute as the other. Nate shook my hand. "'*I'm sorry my dumbass brother hit you in the face.*'" Before I could respond, Evan whispered, "'*I'm not.*'"

"I desperately wanted Evan to walk me home, just like in the movies, but I knew he couldn't. My dad would've flipped out, and I really wanted to see Evan again. He wrote his number on my hand and begged me not to wash it off. There was no way I was going to. I held my hand away from my body, not wanting to smear his handwriting as I rushed home. I tore through my house, running up the stairs to my room to find a piece of paper. My room was still in boxes, and my hand started to sweat. I started to panic. I was so afraid I'd lose his number. I tore through two or three boxes, I don't remember how many, until I found a piece of paper and pressed my hand down to transfer his number. That was something I had thought romantic."

I pull at my bottom lip, remembering that day clearly. My heart had never beaten so fast before. A soft smile forms against my will as the image of an old piece of paper tucked in the corner of my dresser comes to mind.

"Funny thing, I still have that paper tucked in my dresser drawer."

FOUR

Evan

THE THERAPIST STANDS AND walks over to her window to close the blinds. "Is that better?"

I nod, not realizing the sun was shining on my face until she pulled the string. I attempt to relax, but the truth is I'm on edge. I don't see how she's going to fix anything today, tomorrow or even next month.

"The late afternoon sun can be blinding."

"Why not change around your office?"

Her eyes wander as if she's considering my suggestion. I know she's not though. You can tell by the faded carpet my feet rest on that the furniture hasn't moved probably since the doors opened. If I didn't know better, I'd say her lifestyle is a lot like mine – stationary and afraid of change. Ryley is the exact opposite. Every time I visited her dorm room, it was different from the last time. Her and her roommate's beds would be swapped around and there'd be new posters or other decorations hanging on the walls. I once told her that one night I was going to sneak in and end up in the wrong bed. I laughed but she didn't think it was that funny.

"I'm not a fan of change," she says, confirming my assumption.

"Yeah, me neither."

"I find that surprising since you're in the military."

I set my arms on the arm rest and lean slightly forward. "Being in the military doesn't eliminate my aversion to change. When I was growing up, my father was adamant that everything stayed the same. Our couch was always in the same location and was only moved so we could clean underneath it, and even then it was set back down in the same exact location. Not an inch off in either direction. When I came home on leave the first time, I went to throw my bag – like I had done many times – onto the couch only for it to land on the newly purchased coffee table that shattered into pieces. My mom was pissed, but I told her that the couch hadn't moved in eighteen years so how did I know?"

"A lot has changed for you over the past few years though?"

I sit back and nod. "Not by choice."

"Surely some of it was by choice. You entered the service under your own free will, did you not?"

"I did. I also chose my field, but I didn't choose to be gone so long or miss the birth of my son. Those weren't choices I made. They were done for me. I'm not choosing to sit here, but I'm here for Ryley and I'll do anything for her." I have to look away. I don't want her to see the pain and anger in my eyes. For years, I've fought to get back here and each and every time we thought we were close. Each and every time we thought a unit would be waiting for us. They weren't.

"Do you have trust issues, Evan?"

"Yes and no," I mumble.

"Care to expand?"

Not really, but I know I have to. "I shouldn't trust the Navy, but I do. I don't know what to think and Nate's on a mission, so it's not like I can sit down and ask him." I shrug. "I'm not even sure he'll tell me the truth. He took my girl when he was supposed to be keeping me alive in her heart.

It's the Navy that has protected me for years, yet kept me away from my life. They kept me alive so I could return home, but part of me wonders why it took so long and how much Nate really knew."

"Why do you think Nate's lying?"

The thought of Nate and Ryley together turns my blood cold. I want to kill him. If he was in my unit, he'd be dead for touching something that doesn't belong to him. I stand abruptly, knocking over the chair, and start to pace. My hands rub roughly over my face, and I let out a growl of frustration.

"Evan?"

I shake my head to let her know I'm not ready. I lean my head against the wall and try to think about anything other than Ry and Nate together, but I can't. Since I came home, they're all I see. I want to forget he's my brother and destroy him, but knowing my mom has lost so much holds me back. He and I will never be brothers again though, that's for sure. I'll never be able to forget what he's done.

"He's always liked her," I say quietly.

"How does that make you feel?"

I close my eyes and picture him watching her while she sat on our couch, waiting for me to come home. He was so enthralled with her he didn't even hear me come in.

"There was this time I walked into the family room. They hadn't heard me come in so I took a moment to just watch, observe. I stood in the doorway with my eyes on Ryley. She was sitting cross-legged with her book in her lap. She was always doing homework and that benefited me because she'd make sure I did mine too. When we started dating, my grades went up. I didn't care that she was smarter than me. She was the beauty, and I was the brawn; it made us work. Standing there, watching her, I was jealous of the pen that she held in her mouth while reading her book.

"When I looked to my left, there was Nate sitting in our dad's chair. He had an open book in his lap, but his eyes weren't focused on his reading material. They were on Ryley. I knew that look – I got it every time I stared at her – but I didn't like seeing it on his face." I shake my head remembering the look on his face when I caught him. "I cleared my throat and he jumped. Only guilty people jump. He knew I had caught him gawking at my girl."

I turn and face her. She looks poised and ready for whatever I'm about to throw at her. "I never doubted Ryley's love for me when we were younger. Hell, not even while I was away. I trusted her. That was the one thing I could take with me when I deployed. She loved me, supported me, and I knew she'd be waiting for me when I stepped off that plane to come home. When Nate was home I knew they spent time together, but now I question everything. What were they doing? How long has this been going on? I leave and come back to nothing. My life – the one I was counting on being there waiting for me with open arms – is in the arms of my brother. The one man I was relying on has taken my family away from me. He was supposed to protect what's mine, not covet it. I never thought in a million years he'd make a move on Ryley."

I walk over to the water cooler and fill a paper cup. I have to do this repeatedly to quench my thirst. She offered me a mug when I walked in, but I don't know how well it's been cleaned. I crush the cup in my hand and toss it in the wastebasket before returning to my chair.

"I feel angry and betrayed," I say, finally answering her question. "I feel as if my whole life with Ryley has been one big lie, and I'm not sure if I can ever shake that feeling."

"But you trust her?"

My head moves slowly up and down, as if it's unsure of my answer. "I do trust her, more than anything, but I can't wrap my head around why she'd go to Nate."

"Evan, sometimes love has an odd way of working around pain."

I lean forward and look her square in the eye. "What about my pain? What about my agony? Who's going to nurse my heartbreak? How come these thoughts weren't going through either of their heads when they started betraying me like this? How come he wasn't scouring the ends of the earth looking for me? Someone knew we were alive out there, and no one came."

She picks up her pen and scribbles on her notepad. I don't even care what she's writing. I just want to be done so I can go drown my sorrows at Magoo's. At least my favorite bartender is still working, *Slick Rick*. Thank God some things never change.

"Do you feel like Ryley betrayed you?"

"Yes." My words sting, but they're the truth.

FIVE

Ryley

"DID YOU CALL HIM?"

I finish off my water and set the glass on the table beside the couch. My fingers linger on the wood. The table feels worn and old. The wood is rough and in need of refinishing. I imagine it's from years of water stains and wet tissues being left there from the many sessions before mine.

That's how my life feels right now, worn and old. The vibrancy I once knew is no longer there. I'm reduced to memories, hard stares and what if's. I spend most of my time with my arms crossed, holding in my heart because I know it's going to burst out of my chest any moment now. Bringing up these memories is painful.

I shake my head. "I tried, but I think when you're sixteen and you've just been mesmerized by someone who, in your mind, is the epitome of a romance novel character, you become tongue-tied. I picked up the phone many times and pressed six of the seven digits needed, but could never press the last one. Each time I'd put my phone back on its cradle, held my head in my hands and chided myself for being stupid. He gave me his number. He wants me to call. That's what I told myself over and over again.

"Before I knew it, it was dark, and I was still sitting on the edge of my bed with my pink phone laughing at me, the boxes in my room mocking me. My knees had been bent for so long they screamed in agony when I moved. I had chickened out and convinced myself that Evan was just a dream. That Evan Archer didn't exist, even though my heart knew he did.

"The next day was my first day of school. I should've been excited, but I wasn't. The only thing I wanted to do was get through my day, act like I didn't exist and rush home to sit on my bed and try calling Evan. My plan was to call while he was still at school, wherever that was, and leave a message. That way I didn't have to talk to anyone, especially his mom. I don't know why, but the thought of asking for her son to come to the phone scared the ever-loving daylights out of me.

"Being the new kid in school was something I was used to. My mom's job moved us a lot, so fitting in was a piece of cake. I knew the routine: keep your head held high, smile and never sit in the front of the class. That was actually the first thing I learned. You never want to come off as too eager to learn and be the teacher's pet. My first class of the day was AP Honors English. I chose the fourth seat in the third row. I remember I had to look busy so as not to draw attention to myself, but I looked to my left when the seat next to me shifted.

"I was met with those ocean blue eyes and a smile that made me forget my name. Only it wasn't Evan. It took me a moment to realize the similarities between Evan and Nate, but once I did, there wasn't anything stopping my verbal vomit."

"'*You look just like your brother.*'" I blurted out the words with such embarrassment, but he didn't care. His eyes shone with humor, and he laughed. I wasn't sure what he found so funny because I felt like an idiot for saying what I did. Siblings often look like each other, but Evan and Nate were almost too similar. I was too wrapped up in Evan the night before to realize that they're twins. They weren't the first set of twins I've met, but Evan and Nate were different. They weren't identical because you could tell them apart, but from a distance, you'd never know who was coming at you. Both are tall with dark hair and beautiful blue eyes, but when they were side by side, you could tell them apart. Evan has the most adorable dimples and Nate has a slightly crooked nose from breaking it during football. Where Evan has straight hair, Nate's is wavy and the girls in school always loved his hair. Nate was always skinnier than Evan too, even though they worked out the same. Evan could put on muscle like he was taping it to himself. I know that upset Nate.

"'We're twins, and you just made the other me very happy.'" Nate said this with such excitement. It dawned on me quickly that Evan was in this school with me, and that I'd see him.

"'Why's that?'" I hadn't a clue what I was doing, but Nate seemed to appreciate that. He pulled out his cell phone and an instant wave of envy washed over me. I wanted a cell phone, but my father wouldn't allow it. I thought for sure with us living off base and me attending a public school, he'd get me one. It didn't matter how much I pouted, he said no each time.

"'Evan has been pacing by the phone waiting for you to call. He's going to be outside that door when the bell rings now that he knows you're here.'" My eyes went instantly to the door and to the clock, back and forth until the big-hand was on the seven. I thought that I was going to burst out of my chair when the bell rang, but I didn't. Somehow I moved with such precision and calmness that I was the last one out of the class."

"Was Evan there waiting for you?" she asks with just as much excitement as Nate had that day in his voice.

"He was. When I walked out of the classroom he was standing across from me. His leg was bent with his foot pressed up against the locker. His hand was resting on his bent leg, his books resting on his thigh. He beckoned me with his finger, and I moved toward him as if he was pulling me by a string. I thought, 'Wow, a real-life James Dean, and he wants to talk to me.'

"'*You didn't call.*'"

"'*I chickened out.*'"

I shake my head, pulling my bottom lip into my mouth. I sigh, remembering my first day of school. "I couldn't believe I had just said that, but he didn't care. His eyes were soft and welcoming. Evan was an easy one to read, a very open book. His hand sought out mine, his fingers weaving, locking us in place. He was holding my hand again, a thought that I couldn't even begin to put into words."

"'*Can I walk you to your next class?*'"

"Did you let him?" she asks, almost too eager to hear our love story.

I stand and take my empty glass to the water cooler. Right now I feel brave enough to talk about Evan when we were in high school. I don't want to talk about Evan and the past six years though. Those memories are painful. I fill my glass and walk back to the once royal blue couch and sit down. I tuck my legs up underneath me and rest my arm on the side. My fingers pick at the threads that have come loose.

"I did, every day until he graduated. He was seventeen when we met and starting his senior year."

"When was your first date?"

"Technically that day. He asked me to stay after school until his football practice was over so he could walk me home. I was afraid my dad would be upset with a strange boy walking with me, but it was a risk I was willing to take. I'm a romantic at heart and believe in love at first sight. I was in love with Evan Archer, and if he asked me to jump off a bridge for him I probably would've done it."

"That's extreme, Ryley. Are you always that intense with your emotions?"

"It's how he made me feel. The sun was brighter. The clouds were bigger. The birds even sang louder once I met him. I know not everyone has that experience, but I did. He was like my daily dose of life."

"Interesting. Please continue with your first date."

I nod. This lady doesn't forget anything. "Our first date happened while he was walking me home. He kept apologizing for hitting me with the football and asked if he could make it up to me. I wasn't going to tell him 'no' so we stopped at this little ice cream shop. He asked if he could order for me, and I told him that would be fine. I went and picked a table for us to sit. When he came to the table, he asked me to close my eyes. Of course, I did. What I didn't expect was for him to feed me the first bite followed by our first kiss.

"Evan placed the spoon at my lips, and I opened my mouth. The chocolate and raspberry combination was heaven. I knew right away what he had chosen. But the best part was when he replaced the spoon with his lips. My cold lips met his..." my fingers run softly over my lower lip as I remember the feeling of him being there. "Do you know how people say certain emotions cause you to see fireworks?"

The therapist nods.

"I was the firework. I was the butterfly. I was every analogy you could think of. I didn't see stars. I became the star. My first kiss was everything it was meant to be and more."

SIX

Evan

———

"I WANT TO SHIFT gears and talk about some happier times for you."

"Okay," I reply, picking up the chair that I had knocked over. I lean over and clutch the arm rest as my mind pictures them splintering apart from my grip. I want to break everything in my sight, or shoot something and watch as the bullet rips through and decimates its framework. She makes me want to talk, even if it's against my will. I don't know if it's her voice or the fact that I know Ryley was here earlier, sitting in this same room and answering the same questions that allow the words to flow freely through my lips.

My thoughts drift to the couch, and I find myself wondering if Ryley sat there or in this chair. Did she lie down and relax? Or sit rigid like me? It's been so long since I've been in a room with her I don't want to think about how she's changed. I know she's not the same woman I left behind, and I can't deny that I want the same girl I fell in love with. I want her to run into my arms and tell me that everything is going to be okay even though I was the one always saying those words to her.

"Tell me about the time you met Ryley."

I chuckle and release the armrests, walking around to the front of the chair. I sit down with a huff. "She didn't tell you?"

The therapist sets her pen down and clasps her hands together. She smiles lightly, telling me that yes Ryley did, in fact, fill her in. I love that the way we met brings a smile to a stranger's face. Yes, the woman across from me is a stranger, regardless of what she's learned from Ryley. It's a story I love to tell though, so I'm happy to oblige.

"Evan, you know I can't tell you what Ryley and I discussed today, and I'll be honest, I'll likely use some of the information I learned earlier to see where you're at." She leans back, allowing her chair to rock back and forth. "I've been a couple's therapist for years now and while it can be frustrating, it can also be rewarding. When Ryley presented your case I knew that I'd have to do a different approach and that time was of the essence."

My eyes drop down when she brings up time. I know that there's a time limit, that Ryley is being pressured. I didn't ask her to bring us here, but I'm not going to lie; if this works I'll be grateful. I also know she's set to walk down the aisle shortly and everything in me is telling me that I'll be there to stop it. She's supposed to be marrying me, not him. It's never been him.

"Evan, are you still with me?"

I look up quickly and blink away the vision of Ryley in a white dress carrying a bouquet of her favorite flowers, her arm locked inside of her father's as they walk down the carpeted floor to where I should be waiting for her. I don't want to know how this daydream plays out because I could very well not be standing there waiting for her. It could be Nate and if that's the case I'm either dead again, or I've lost her. I know she feels that she lost me and if I could, I'd go back and change history. But I can't. All I can do is provide her with the answers I have and maybe together we can put the puzzle pieces back together and see if we still fit.

"Yeah, sorry." I clear my throat and sit up a bit straighter. "When I met Ryley I was this cocky teen who thought my shit didn't stink, but boy was I wrong. I never had any trouble getting a girlfriend, and I really never wanted one, but the girls flocked to me and I let them until I met Ry.

"The guys and I were hanging out at the park playing a little football, when for some reason I cocked my arm back and threw this long pass." I imitate the throwing motion much to the therapist's surprise. Her eyes go wide as she bring her hands up in front of her face as if she's going to catch my pass. For the first time, I laugh at the humor present in the room.

"Sorry," I say as I bring my arm back down to my side. I rub my hands on my pants and remember the day I was graced with Ryley entering my life.

"'*Holy shit, what the hell did you do, Archer?*'" I stood in the open field with my mouth agape, ignoring the condescending voice behind me. When I let the ball free from my hand I knew it was going to sail over everyone's head, but I had no idea it would land across the street and knock someone out. I remember I said 'shit' as I saw her fall to the ground. I thought my dad was going to kill me for hitting her with the football. The last thing I wanted was for him to come down on my ass and threaten military school. That was his answer to everything. He went, so he figured his sons needed the same education.

"The closer I got, the faster time slowed down. I've never felt time stop and I've never seen a ripple, but I swear that's what happened. I knelt down in front of my poor, unsuspecting victim and touched her arm. I teetered at the zap that coursed through my arm when my fingers touched her skin. Still to this day, I know I can feel the residual pain.

"Her hair, it was red from the sunlight and covering her face. I knew without a shadow of a doubt that once she moved her hair, I'd be done for.

"As soon as she looked at me, even though it was through one eye because her hand was concealing the damage that I had done, I swallowed hard. My father was going to kill me, but death was going to be my reprieve because she was an angel and was definitely going to be my demise. When I pulled her hand away from her angelic face, my shoulders slumped. I had hurt her.

"I remember looking back at the guys, each one of them standing on the sideline, half of them without shirts on and the only thing going through my mind was that I didn't want her to see them. I wanted her to only see me. They started yelling for me to throw the football back. 'Stupid assholes,' I said after throwing it back across the street. I wasn't ready to leave so I knelt back down in front of this goddess that I tried to kill and tried, for the life of me, to smile sexy.

"'*Shit, babe, I've gone and messed up your pretty face.*'" Of course the first words she ever heard me say were cuss words. I should've kicked myself in the nuts. I was such a fumbling fool in those moments, but the one thing I did that felt right was take her hand in mine. The intense feeling I had when I touched her earlier was much stronger. I never wanted to let go."

I cover my face and fight the emotions coursing through me. "The moment I saw her, I was a goner. No one else existed or could even hold a candle to what Ryley meant to me. Anyway, I took her over to meet the guys and ended up playing like crap the rest of the day. We called the game early because I wasn't into it. I just wanted to sit with her and find out what made her tick. I wanted to walk her home that night, but she said her parents wouldn't like it. I hated watching her leave, but she assured me she'd be fine. For the first time ever, I wrote my number on a girl's hand. I ran home, even though Nate and I drove that day. I don't think I had ever run that fast in my life, but I needed to be home waiting, when she called.

"My brother found me in the morning slumped over with my head resting on my arms next to the telephone."

"But fate intervened."

"Ah yeah, fate was something fantastic the next day when Nate texted and told me that she was in his class. That was my second chance, and I wasn't going to mess it up. I didn't know what I was doing, it was almost unchartered territory for me, but I was going to give it the ole Boy Scout try."

"What exactly?"

I adjust in my seat, but don't even try to hide the smile appearing on my face. "I was going to woo the girl and make her mine. I was going to work to show her that I wasn't some dumb jock who couldn't control his throwing arm. I was going to show Ryley that I was worth the bruise she was proudly displaying."

"And how were you going to do that, Evan?"

"With ice cream, of course."

SEVEN

Ryley

THE THERAPIST SHUFFLES SOME papers on her desk. She knows I'm lost in thought remembering my first kiss with Evan. My first best kiss, the one kiss to leave me speechless. It was my secret and no one would know that the very dreamy Evan Archer was my first kiss. However, in my head, I was screaming it from the rooftops. Yes, that was my best secret first kiss.

I need a break, mentally at least. I stand, walk over to the window and see Lois' car in the same place she parked it earlier. It's somewhat calming to know that she's on the other side of the door waiting for me. My eyes drift over to the park, and there sits Evan on the bench facing the window. He doesn't look up, but maybe if I pound on the glass he will. I know he's hurting. Our lives have been turned upside down and ripped apart too many times to count. He hates that he doesn't have the answers to solve our problems. No one does. I'm not even sure why I'm here. What is she going to say or do to give me the solution I need? Everything's a mess.

Evan looks up, and even from this distance I know he's not smiling. I pick my hand up to wave, but immediately drop it, afraid of giving him false hope. Afraid of giving myself false hope.

"Evan," I whisper his name as if I'm the only one in the room. I know I'm breaking his heart and he knows he's broken mine, even if he didn't mean to. We need life to be as simple as the movies or a board game. Spin the dial to determine your job. Spin again and move forward five spots to get married. I want to spin and spin again until every decision is made for me. I want someone or something to tell me which path I'm supposed to follow.

"What about Nate?" she asks. I also smile at the mention of Nate's name. I rest my head against the window and watch Evan. His head is in his hands, a sure sign that he's in deep thought. I want to go to him and hold him. I want to pretend that we're the characters in one of my beloved books and that when we get to the last chapter, everything we are meant to be will be.

Sadly, my life is anything but a romance novel and as I stand here, watching the man I love while engaged to his brother, my thoughts filter to Nate. He doesn't have a clue what's going on and I can't call him. I can't pick up the phone and say, 'when you come home everything's changed.' He thinks his brother is dead. It's what we've been told for the past six years. It's how we've lived.

I say his name over and over in my head. He's been my rock for so long, and I don't know how I'm going to break this news to him.

I shake my head not understanding her question.

"When did you become close?"

I sigh. "We've always been close. Nate was in most of my classes. At first, Evan was jealous because Nate and I were always studying, but eventually he got over it. I was always with Evan and if I wasn't, Nate was around. Life seemed to work out that way. Being with them made me happy."

"And now?"

I turn away from the window. "And now things are complicated. Nate is on a mission, and I don't know when he'll be back. Sometimes he's gone for a day, other times it's a month. If I have a problem, he's the one who guides me. I don't know what I'm supposed to do here, and it's only going to get worse when Nate comes home. I'm not naïve enough to think you're giving me the answers when I walk out of here, and it's not like I can Google my question and have an array of answers guiding me."

I run my hand through my hair, pulling at my ponytail. I lean against the wall, still able to see Evan. He used to smile so brightly, but now it's dull and faded. The light has gone from him, from us, all because of some miscommunication. Things didn't have to be like this.

"Do you love him?"

I smile when she asks this. "I do, with everything that I am. He's been my rock, my foundation. He's my best friend. He's my lover. Without him, I'm a hollow shell of who I used to be. He rebuilt me from ground up. We didn't intend to fall in love. Well, I didn't at least, but being in love with Nate is easy. He's been my best friend for so long that my feelings just grew. He was a constant support in my life and as much as I didn't want to ruin our friendship, the blurred line had already been crossed in my heart. Falling for Nate was as easy as falling for Evan in some ways."

"What do you mean?"

"He's been in love with me since we met, but he never said anything because of Evan. I found out a year after Evan... I heard Nate and Carter arguing. The conversation wasn't meant for my ears and for weeks I didn't speak to Nate, but I couldn't continue not seeing him. I needed him."

"And who's Carter?"

"He's Nate's best friend and Lois' husband."

The therapist nods and scribbles on her pad. It makes me

wonder what she's writing or thinking. Her questions are one-liners and she's yet to offer me any guidance.

"What was Nate like in high school?"

"Smart, funny and athletic. He always had girls chasing after him because he was going 'somewhere'. He was definitely the type that you bring home to your mom. I didn't like most of the girls he went out with and used to make their little sister torment his dates. I know it was childish, but no one ever seemed good enough for him.

"The twins – that's what I called them when they were together – both played football. Evan was the running back and Nate was the quarterback, which explains how I ended up with a black eye from Evan throwing the ball. Their coach called them a deadly combination because they each knew what the other was thinking. In the winter they moved on to basketball and in the spring, baseball. They were three-sport varsity athletes and I didn't miss a single game that year. For the away games I would ride with their mom, and we'd stand there and cheer our hearts out for our boys.

"Anyway, Nate was every good girl's dream. He was voted most likely to succeed in high school."

"And did he?" she asks.

"He did, until Evan… They both joined the Navy after high school and quickly went up the ranks. It's hard to become a SEAL, but both of them did it. Everyone was proud of what they were accomplishing. It was hard not to be. Evan and Nate set a goal and they both achieved it. After Evan, Nate took his bereavement leave to stay with me, but he too was struggling with Evan's death. We talked about the how's and why's. Most of the time we just sat and stared at his picture. Evan's death was hard for Nate to take and he kept watching for the conflict to appear on television. He was glued to the news day in and day out. I finally told him to go back to base, to be there and listen. Maybe someone would say something about Evan's unit."

"How did you feel about Nate returning to active duty?"

I shrug. "I grew up on different bases, so I get it. My mom's military, but not in combat. My grandfather was though, so I've heard the stories. There's pride in their voices when they talk. I know it's in your blood and these men and women – the ones that yearn to defend their country – they do it proudly."

"You had grown close to Nate after Evan died in combat. How did you feel about Nate leaving again?"

"Scared and helpless, but he had to do it. I couldn't sit by and watch him miss that piece of him. He'd already lost his father and brother, but didn't need to lose his family too." I take one last look at Evan before heading back to the couch. "His mother, she's not speaking to me and his sister hates me."

"Why's that?"

I smirk and shake my head. "She's lost her husband and son, and I was giving her remaining son an open invitation to return to combat. She told me that if I loved him and Evan the way I say I do, I'd be more determined to keep him home. She didn't like that I told her being in combat made him happy, complete. And his sister… she lost her dad, lost her brother and thinks that I'm evil incarnate because Nate and I are engaged. It's messy. Our family life is complicated. Standing in the middle of all of this is EJ, and he doesn't have a clue."

"And who's EJ?"

My smile spreads from ear to ear as EJ's image pops into my mind. My red-headed blue-eyed little boy who's a spitting image of his dad in every way possible. Everyone thinks he looks like me, but I see nothing but his dad in him.

"EJ is my son." I leave it at that. The rest – it's hard to grasp.

"Who's his father?"

"Well now, that's where one of my problems lies, isn't it? Evan is my son's biological father, but he knows Nate as his dad. I don't know how to look my little boy in the eye and tell him that the dad he knows isn't his dad and that the man he's named after is. How do I answer the question of why or where Evan has been when the answer doesn't even make sense to me? How am I supposed to do that?"

This time I can't hold back the tears. Telling EJ, at the age of five, that his life is a lie isn't something I planned on doing until he was old enough to understand the sacrifices Evan's made for our country. At five, EJ should be worried about trucks, and mud and what girl he likes in his kindergarten class, not who his father is.

EIGHT

Evan

THE MEMORY OF OUR first date is so vivid that it feels like yesterday. The way Ryley closed her eyes as the spoon touched her lips had me moving closer to her, and I just about lost my nerve when I saw her tongue inch out so slowly to taste the raspberry and chocolate that waited for her. I knew in that moment, that I'd kiss her. I just didn't expect it to be as earth shattering as it was. For the first time my heart was beating and it was all because of her.

"How did you feel when you enlisted?"

I stretch out my legs in front of me. I glance at the clock and notice I've only been here for fifteen minutes. It seems like an hour has passed. My time should be up. I should be standing and walking out, never to see this lady again. Instead, she's seated across from me with her hands folded neatly on top of her desk. Her posture is relaxed and that's meant to be comforting. I'm anything but.

Her question takes me by surprise, and it's something I love talking about. I'm proud to serve my country, always have been. Even in light of what I've learned this past week, I'm still serving.

"I was excited. I had looked at various colleges for about a year. I had a few scholarship offers, but I never felt a connection with any of them. My dad wasn't too thrilled that I had decided to enlist. I think he thought I'd go to college since Nate was heading off to the Navy. I had always been more into sports while Nate was always learning from my dad. I got the impression when I enlisted that he thought I was trying to steal Nate's thunder."

"Why do you think that was?"

I lean my head back slightly and close my eyes. Telling my father that I was enlisting in the Navy did not go over well. Nate had broken the news first, and I saw how happy my dad was. I thought for sure he'd accept my decision to enlist as well. Only he didn't. When I said the word 'enlist' he frowned, and when I said 'Navy', he downright grimaced. It was only after his passing did I learn that he wanted me to play ball in college and thought I was wasting my talent. That, coupled with the fact that I had chosen the same path as Nate, meant that he was none too happy with me. He wanted something different for me.

"It was Ry's dad who sold me on the military. They were having a barbeque and he had some buddies there. Her dad was Army, but never favored one branch over the other. He was always very accepting. I sat and listened to their stories and just became mesmerized. One of them hinted that he was a little more than Special Forces. He detailed the history of this unit and everything that they did, and I could see myself jumping out of planes in the middle of a firefight. I could see myself serving the people we were trying to protect. I wanted that thrill, that danger, but I didn't want to wait. One suggested the Navy and mentioned the SEALs, saying you can go to school after basic. That's what I wanted."

I look down at my leg and tap my thumb and forefinger against the crease in my slacks. Everything back then seemed so simple. Sign my name on the dotted line and serve my country. My goal was to make a name for myself, marry Ryley and raise a family.

"Evan?"

I look up at the sound of my name being called. I clear my throat and sit up. "I'm sorry," I say. "I zoned out."

"Care to share what you were thinking about?"

I shake my head, my lips pursing. Some of these memories, they're painful. It makes me miss everything that's happened in Ryley's life these past six years. I know it's not possible to miss something you didn't have or know about, but I do. I want to be fresh in her memories, and right now I'm nothing but a ghost.

"Your father died in combat, correct?"

My eyes move toward the window – the same window that I know Ryley stood at earlier and watched as I sat on the park bench. Even from a distance, I could see the anguish she was going through because of me. Too many times I stood with the intent of just leaving, anything to ease the pain I've caused, but I can't walk away, not now. Ryley and I didn't do anything wrong in this fucked up mess. We deserve a chance.

"Like most, his death was a result of 9/11." I shake my head lightly. So many deaths and the war will never end. "He was working with some ground troops. They were clearing out a village and one of the soldiers on his first deployment wasn't watching where he was walking. The IED took out about six of them, my dad included.

"Nate and I were the first to know. He was in Iraq, and I had just landed in Afghanistan. Even though my dad and I were in the same country, we didn't see each other. At least not the way we thought." I look down at the floor and focus on the hole in the carpet wondering how long the patch has been bare.

"My dad bled out in the field, his legs were blown away

from his body. The medic said he didn't suffer, but he was alive for a few minutes after the blast. At first I believed the medic, but as I saw my own combat and watched my friends die, I know his ears were ringing and he could hear the yelling even if it was muffled. He knew what was going on as his breathing became labored and he couldn't feel his legs. I know he fought to move before insurgents could move in on their position. I've seen it over and over again. The soldiers who aren't injured are scrambling to save their comrades all while trying to save themselves."

I have to get up and walk. Flashes of soldiers down on the ground are images I don't want to recall right now. I run my hand through my hair and tug at the ends lightly. I sigh heavily and rest my head against the wall. "War is ugly. It destroys families and your faith in humanity. I lost my dad and had to let my sister grow up without a man in the house. Nate and I could've taken a discharge, but my mom assured us they were fine."

I shake my head and move back to the chair, but before sitting down I look at the therapist and take her in. She's not writing or even watching me, but crying. She sheds tears for a family she doesn't even know, a man who lost his life serving his country.

She catches me watching her and tries to smile. She pulls a tissue from her the box that sits on top of her desk and dries her eyes. I'm taken by her ability to show emotion with a job like hers. I have to look away because I don't want to see the pity in her eyes. My family has been through something no one should ever have to experience because of war.

"Are you ready to talk about what happened to you the last time you deployed?"

My eyes study her, sharply. My head moves before I have time to think because no, I don't want to talk about the decisions that were made that kept me from my family. That kept three of my unit-mates and me in the dense forest for years without communication, surviving only on our skills while trying to find the most elusive man in the world.

"We'll have to discuss your time there."

"Not right now," I demand. "I'll talk about anything else, but that."

NINE

Ryley

_____

"HOW SOON DID YOU and Evan start dating?"

I fold my hands in my lap and think back to those first days of school. "If you were to ask Evan, he'd say it's the day we first kissed. It's something we used to argue about all the time, but for me I think it was the first day he told another girl that he had a girlfriend. He had never said that word to me before, and I didn't want to assume."

"Why not?"

I shrug. "He had other girlfriends before me, and I thought he just went around kissing girls in ice creams shops. I don't know. I didn't want to believe that he had chosen me and I had all these questions."

"Like what, Ryley?"

"Like, why me? I wasn't anything special, and I was new. Evan had his pick of any girl in that school and he chose me. It made me wonder a lot and second guess his intentions."

"I think that's common among teenagers," she says. I silently agree with her.

I sit up a bit straighter on the couch and smooth out my dress. "About two or three weeks into the school year, I was walking down the hall to my next class. It was right next to

Evan's locker, so I knew I'd see him. His back was facing me when I walked around the corner, but I could see that he was with a blond. I didn't know her, but had seen her around campus a few times. I stopped, not intending to eavesdrop, but more to brace myself for what I thought I was going to see."

The therapist leans forward. Is my story exciting to her?

"What did you see?"

"Nothing," I say, shaking my head. "It's what I heard. She was asking him to go to homecoming with her, and he said he was taking his girlfriend. She asked who he was dating because she hadn't heard and when he said my name... it was like my heart was trying to take over my body. It was beating so hard. I couldn't catch my breath. I gasped so loudly. I was embarrassed. He turned around with this boyish grin on his face, and I knew he was talking about me."

"Evan sounds romantic."

"He was..." I fiddle with the end of my dress before dropping it back in place and folding my hands. "I'm sure, if given the opportunity, he still is. He's very unassuming."

"What do you mean by unassuming, Ryley?"

"Evan came off as the dumb jock type to his friends. He was always laughing and goofing off in the halls or after school. He never took anything seriously. If there was a big game or a championship game he was the one cracking jokes all day to ease everyone's tension. He was the life of the party, except when we were alone."

"What was he like then?"

A single tear drops. "Sweet, caring and loving. He taught me what it felt like to be loved. To be worshipped. He taught me, well, everything. I was this naïve girl who had her first kiss in an ice cream shop, but that didn't seem to bother him. He didn't see me as a challenge or a conquest. He never made fun of me because of my lack of experience. The way he made me feel... I still felt that way the day he left for his last deployment."

"When did Evan first leave you?"

"It was the beginning of my junior year in college when he called and said he was leaving. I knew the day was coming, but never thought I'd actually hear him say those words.

"*'Hi, babe.'*"

"*'Hi.'*"

"*'I have to leave for a little bit.'*"

"*'Where?'*"

"*'Oh, you know, Ry. I'm going to go protect our country, but don't worry though. I'll be back.'*"

"The next day, I went to the base and filled out some paperwork. The secretary said I was lucky because most of the single men leave everything to their moms and that he must really love me. I told her I didn't want the money just him. The one thing I wouldn't get was his death benefit; that was strictly next of kin, and until we were married that wasn't me.

"I didn't even want the life insurance, but I wasn't going to tell him that. Anyway, we had a week until he left, and I was a mess, but not in front of him. I'd break down in the bathroom or in between classes. It was weird because I didn't see him every day, but knowing he was an hour away made things a little easier for me. Knowing that I'd see him on the weekends was like my reward for doing well in school.

"So with a deadline looming, I was a wreck. All I could think about is what if he doesn't come home or what if he comes home and doesn't want me anymore? So many thoughts were running through my mind, but I couldn't share them with him. I couldn't put him under that stress. I needed him to leave with a clear head and with the knowledge that I loved him more than anything.

"I hid a lot of my fears from him for years. I just couldn't bring myself to tell him what I was feeling. I think, sometimes, he thought I knew how to deal with deployment because of my dad, but that was different."

"What happened the day he left?"

"It was a beautiful day, and I woke up in his arms. He could've gotten into trouble, but he didn't care. It wasn't the weekend so no visitors were allowed in the barracks, but he was all for breaking the rules that night."

"*It's time for me to go.*"

"*I know.*"

"His kisses were gentle, not rushed. He was memorizing the way we fit. I started crying against my will. I couldn't hold my tears back. I didn't want him to go. I was used to having him on my weekends and now he was going to be gone for who knows how long... a year or longer. I was just so afraid that we wouldn't be the same when he came back."

"*I love you, Ry. I love you so damn much nothing's going to change that. I'm going to come home to you and get you to walk down the aisle to marry my sorry ass.*"

"*I love you too, Evan. Please come home to me.*"

"*I promise.*"

"He promised every time he left, and I believed him." I wipe away a tear, keeping my eyes on the ground. "I felt fear when he was gone. In the blink of an eye everything changed. Nothing prepares you for them leaving even though you know it's coming. Phones calls don't stop until they're on the plane and you're left standing there wondering what the hell just happened. Some wives cry hysterically and others – the ones that have done this many times – shed a few tears, round up their children and head back to their homes to start a new routine.

"The wives had each other. I didn't have anyone. I was going back to school to finish out my year. Evan would miss my summer vacation. We wouldn't be taking weekend camping trips or going to the beach. I didn't have Nate, either.

He was off doing his own specialized training and that meant I was alone."

"Did Evan call often?"

I shake my head. "The phone calls were sporadic and sometimes I'd miss them because of class or I'd be asleep from studying. With each missed call, I'd cry for days. I just wanted to hear his voice and hear that he was okay. A voice-mail wasn't enough for me. When we could connect, the calls where short and sometimes hard to hear. I tried not to get angry, but I couldn't help it. The littlest things were so impor-tant and we weren't getting those.

"I resorted to writing him letters and sending goodie boxes. I'd go to my parents' on the weekends and make him cookies and buy him necessities. I'd send a box every two weeks, but letters more often. Sometimes the letters were just the words I love you and sometimes it was the essay I had to write for my class. I'd write to him like he was sitting on my bed while I was studying. I sent him pictures of the oddest things, like a random leaf on the ground that fell while I was writing him or something like that. I'd just write so he had words.

"And when letters came in, I didn't want to read them for fear my tears would wash away his words just like the day he gave me his phone number. I needed to hold onto whatever I could until he came home."

"Would you say Evan was possessive of you?"

I laugh. "Yes and no. If you think about it, what teenage boy isn't possessive of what's theirs? But he wasn't violent about it. He did assert himself, but others knew we were together."

"What about other women who were interested in Evan?"

"I had to beat them off with a stick. It was bad. They were everywhere and Nate said it was worse because he had a girlfriend."

"Evan was popular?"

"Both the twins were, but like I said they were different. Evan was outgoing, the life of the party, and his mother called him a skirt chaser. Nate was more academic and just an overall good guy."

"How did you feel when you were with Evan?"

"Secure," I say confidently. Remembering those early days with Evan has helped me keep his memory alive. "Loved. Cherished. I could go on and on." I stop for a minute and look at the therapist. "I know you're probably thinking because his mom called him a skirt chaser that he was a cheater or a womanizer, but he wasn't. Never did I think he was unfaithful to me. He told his dad that once he saw me, no one else existed for him."

"Don't you think he was too young to make that declaration?"

I shake my head and look her square in the eyes. "My parents started dating when they were in the seventh grade. They never dated anyone else and entered the service together and are still happily married. I believe you can find your soul mate at any age; it's the circumstance that brings you together."

"I commend your parents. It's unheard of these days. What can you tell me about Evan and Nate's parents?"

"Um... their dad died a year into the war. The twins enlisted before they graduated and their dad died a year later. It was almost a year to the day from when they signed on the dotted line. They did it because they wanted to follow in their dad's footsteps and because of the terrorist attacks. They wanted to serve with their dad. The Archers were very closed off about their boys though. Nate told me years ago that their father wanted Evan to go to college, to be something different. Nate had made his declaration of enlisting long before Evan did and when Evan went to the recruiter's office, they were eager to have both so the recruiter set everything in motion for them to sign on the same day."

"That's understandable."

"It is and it isn't. Their mom wanted them together, so she was happy. She was always going on about how twins should stick together and that if one was too far, the other would feel the pain. I don't know, the twins are hard to explain. They can finish each other sentences like an old married couple, but at the same time they can be so distant it's unnerving. Archie, their dad, always felt that Nate was in Evan's shadow, and thought this was Nate's time to shine. Anyway, when their dad died, I thought they'd finish out their two years and come home, but they didn't. They both had become SEALs and losing their dad only increased their desire to bring down the enemy."

"How did your parents feel about Evan and you being so close?"

I readjust on the couch, moving to the other side. The cool fabric meets the back of my legs, calming me. "My mom worked a lot more than my dad; he was close to retirement so he was home a lot. After we had ice cream, Evan walked me home and introduced himself to my dad. Evan was raised military so he was very polite when he needed to be, and he charmed my dad big time. But I had rules, and they weren't meant to be broken. For the first month, Evan could come over, but not into the house if neither of my parents were home, so we'd sit on the front porch and drink iced tea. Only when we'd go for a walk or when we'd go to the park, would he sneak kisses. Evan asked my dad if he could take me on a proper date before he asked me. That's how I knew he was serious about me."

"So tell me, do you believe in love at first sight?"

"I do... did. After you've been through what I have, I think you start being cynical and acting detached. You start asking yourself if you loved enough or what you could've done differently. More importantly, you ask yourself if he knew that you loved him more than anything before he died, because you can't bear the thought of him questioning your love for him when he's out there risking his life with bullets flying by his head and his friends lying on the ground with blood coming out of places it shouldn't. I can't..."

"Do you want to take a break, Ryley? How about we take five then we can continue. You're doing great and this isn't about right or wrong answers, this is about finding you."

I nod and get up to use the bathroom. Of course, it's attached to her office so there's no escaping. I close the door and lock it. I'm afraid to look at my reflection in the mirror. The person staring back is not me. This is not who I am. This is not who I want to be. I never thought in a million years that I'd have to make the decision that I'm making now. My life was planned out, it was perfect. I was going to have my house with a big yard so our dog and son could play happily. I was going to meet Evan at the door every night or at the base when he came home from a mission. Everything was going to be fine.

I splash water on my face and dry my hands before heading back into the room. I look at my watch quickly and surmise that I've only been in here for fifteen minutes. It seems like hours, and we've only scratched the surface.

I sit back down and cross my legs. I smile softly, letting her know I'm ready.

"Okay let's try a new topic. You're engaged now?"

I look down at my ring. In a few short weeks I'm to walk down the aisle with only my family present. Nate's mom and sister want to have nothing to do with the ceremony. I understand to an extent, but Evan was gone. Am I not allowed to move on? Is Nate not allowed to love me because of who I am?

"That's why I am here, to see if you can help me sort this mess out, tell me what I should do. Do I marry this man who has been everything to me for the last five years? The man that is the only dad my son – his nephew – knows? Or do I do what is expected, what you see in the movies and go running back into the arms of the man that I love, the man that I was told was dead? That's why I'm here and why he ..." I point to the window where I remember Evan sitting on the other side, waiting for me to make a decision. Everything weighs so heavily on my shoulders. "Evan is out there waiting for me. Waiting for an answer I don't have. Can you just give me the answer?"

"Life isn't a movie, Ryley."

I fight the urge to roll my eyes. "I know it isn't because if it was, I'd hit rewind and start all over. I'd start by telling Evan..."

TEN

Evan

"YOU KNOW, EVAN, SOMETIMES talking about what you've been through makes the outcome easier to deal with."

I adjust, stretching my legs out in front me. This is my relaxed posture, even though I feel rigid as hell and extremely uncomfortable. I had wanted to do this on base, but understood Ryley's reluctance of stepping foot there. The girl I left behind loved the military. She accepted my job into her heart and life with open arms. She encouraged me to be the best, to be better than I thought I could be. Now she wants nothing to do with the Navy, and I can't really blame her. I want everything to do with her though. Not having her in my life, especially since I didn't know she was gone from it to begin with, is unacceptable to me.

"Do you have PTSD?"

My head rises sharply as I glare at her. PTSD isn't something to mess around with and surely if I had it, I wouldn't be talking to a civilian doctor on how to deal with it. Docs on base are trained to deal with who we are when we come home from war or a conflict. I'm not saying she's not, but it's different.

"I wasn't captured or held hostage. It wasn't like that."

53

"What was it like?"

Bringing my legs back up, I lean forward on my knees and clasp my hands together. "Everything I do, everything my unit does, is classified. You get to walk the streets enjoying your freedom because of what we do out there."

"I'm very appreciative of the freedom your actions and those of the military have afforded me as an American." She leans forward making sure she has my attention. "I'm not the enemy here, Evan, I'm here to try and help. I'm here to see if I can give you and Ryley some resolution over the situation. I'm not saying I can, but I'm hoping that by the time we're done here today, you both leave with a path that puts you where you need to be."

"I doubt it," I mumble, looking away from her penetrating gaze.

"You can't fill your mind with doubt, Evan. If you do, it eats at who you are and makes you less of a person. You, Ryley and Nate are in an unfortunate situation, one that can be blamed on a number of people and circumstances."

"I trusted my brother to keep her safe, not get into her pants."

The doctor leans back in her chair and shakes her head. I don't care if she doesn't agree with me. It's what happened. It's how I see things. He knew what I was doing. He had to know we lost communications. It was all written there in my file, and I saw the words written out with my own eyes. Nowhere did it say we were presumed dead. Nowhere did it say we weren't coming home.

"Someone lied to Ryley and to me. Someone has to pay."

"What if that someone is the Navy, Evan? Have you stopped to think about that possibility?"

"Why would they do that?" my voice breaks slightly, showing too much emotion for my liking. I readjust, leaning back. My hands grip the arm rests, waiting for her to elaborate on her theory.

"It may not have been intentional. It could've been a clerical error. I want you to think about all the options here. Was everyone who was assigned to your mission there when you came back? Did anyone leave for a different post, retirement or not reenlist?"

I don't want to think she's right or onto something. We're all professionals, errors like this don't happen. A funeral was had, a body flown back. I'm assuming the CACO showed up on my steps with the chaplain behind him to notify Ryley that I had been killed. Did this happen?

She clears her throat, bringing my attention back to her. "I can sense the wheels turning in your head, Evan. You have a lot of unanswered questions that only your commander can answer for you." The doctor slides a folder over to me, and I watch as it balances on the edge of her desk. I'm almost afraid to pick it up, afraid of the contents inside. Reaching out, I grab the manila folder and open the jacket. Inside is my obituary, along those for my unit members, and other newspaper articles detailing our mission.

"I don't understand."

She sighs, and I can see her moving around through my peripheral vision, but I'm focused on the pages in front of me.

"Here," she says, handing me a cup of water. It's not in one of her mugs and for that I'm thankful. I gulp it down in one swig and wish that it were something stronger to numb away my thoughts. She pulls the folder from my free hand and walks back to her chair. I want to reach over and snatch it back from her. I wasn't done looking at the pieces of newspaper that detail my life's destruction.

"As I said, Evan, not everything is as cut and dry as they've made it out to be. You and your unit were hailed local heroes. You were celebrated and honored. The only thing I can make of it is that someone wanted your unit to disappear. I'm not on the inside, Evan, so I don't know. I can't even assure you that it wasn't your brother, but it wasn't Ryley. It wasn't her or the community that turned their backs on you and your unit."

I have to let her words run their course through my mind and eventually into my heart. What if she's telling the truth? What if this was an inside job that was meant to eliminate our unit? I know I'm not the only one suffering. McCoy came home to find his wife and child gone and hasn't been able to locate them. I suppose I'm the lucky one. My girl was coming home with a bag of groceries when I surprised her. At least she never left our house.

"Do you know anyone in the military?"

Doc shakes her head slowly.

"Everything I say here stays here, right? You're not going to report my session to my CO?"

She leans forward, again piercing me with her eyes. "Evan, everything you say here, in this room or outside with me is protected by doctor-patient confidentiality. Even if I'm subpoenaed, I don't have to answer their questions. We're protected in here."

I nod, fully understanding what she's saying, but I'm not sure if I can bring myself to tell her what happened or how I don't know how everything went so wrong. The mission was an easy one. In and out. A piece of cake. We called it a snatch and grab and figured we'd be home by dinner, relatively speaking.

"Evan, do you want to tell me what kept you away from home for so long?"

ELEVEN

Ryley

"YOU'D START BY TELLING Evan what, Ryley?"

A lone tear finds its way down my cheek. I swipe at it, afraid that more will follow in its wake. There are so many thoughts filtering through my mind that my words are often spoken before I even realize what I'm saying. This would be one of those instances. I spoke too soon. I allowed my words to trail off and she caught meaning behind them.

"Ryley?" she prods in a sweet voice that does nothing to calm me.

"What?" I bite back angrily. She doesn't know what it's like to be me. I had to look Evan in the eye and tell him he's dead to me, to all of us. The words were no sooner out of my mouth before the anger in his eyes flooded me. He didn't understand. Telling that to the man that I loved… a man that I still love even though we buried him years ago. In hindsight, I should've dropped my bags and run into his arms. I should've trailed my fingers over his defined jaw and across his eyelids, confirming what my heart was already telling me. That the love of my life was standing in front of me. That he hadn't died, that we could be whole again. But life had to rear its ugly head and shatter my world even deeper than it had before.

I was cold and standoffish, rude and dismissive. I was everything I shouldn't have been to him because I was scared, shocked and couldn't believe that after so many years he was standing in front of me in flesh and blood, a real-life breathing man who I missed dearly, but I reacted so poorly and all he was expecting was a homecoming, but instead his welcoming party was too confused by his presence.

"Do you need another break?"

I shake my head wildly. It's better that I start talking about Evan more so that when I leave only to come after his session, she can give us some guidance.

"There are a few days that I'd like a re-do on where Evan is concerned. Well probably more than a few, but I'm trying not to be greedy. The day he left, when we were on the tarmac and I held his face in my hands, I told him that I loved him. But what I should've told him is that my love for him runs so deeply that it can never be taken away, that he's who I see when I grow old, sitting by me in a rocking chair and watching the waves crash into the shore. Instead, I kissed him and told him that I loved him because I knew he was coming back.

"When he was there on my front porch, my bags should've dropped. My eggs should've splattered all over my driveway and my gallon of milk should've exploded. Instead, I stood there staring at the ghost who had taken the form of my former fiancé as he descended the stairs of our front porch. His smile was bright, until he saw my face, and then it died.

"I replay that day over and over in my mind. Each scene is the same as I find myself dropping everything and running into his arms. My lips pepper every bit of exposed skin as I tell him over and over again that this can't be real. That he's not real. That every prayer I've uttered for the past six years has come true. I tell him that I love him, and that EJ has missed him so much. In my head, I take his hand in mind, forgetting the groceries scattered all over my driveway, and take him in the house to introduce him to his son. His namesake." I cover my face as tears stream down it. A sob rolls through my body, causing me to choke and gasp for air. I feel her hands on my shoulder, her fingers kneading into my skin trying to comfort me. I'm a despicable human.

"Instead, I told him that I'm engaged to another man. The look…" I cough to clear my throat, in a lame attempt to breathe easier. "The look on his face is something I'll never forget. If he wasn't dead before, I killed him in that moment, shot him down with his own gun."

"Let's take another break, Ryley." Her words are meant to be calming, but they're not. I stand on shaky legs and head to the bathroom. My last few steps are in a sprint as I feel my stomach start to roll. I barely make it before I'm down on my knees and clutching the cold white porcelain for leverage. I dry heave, unable to expel the contents of my stomach. I can't even puke properly right now, that's how messed up I am. Sitting back against the wall and pulling my knees to my chest, I cry into my dress. I've never been more confused than I am now. This session isn't helping, but only showing me how much of a failure I am, and how I did everything wrong.

I should've known better than to let Nate in, but he was there and offered the comfort I so badly needed. He felt the same pain I did. He was going through the same thing I was. He was there when I needed someone to cry to, and it was easy because he understood. He doesn't even know his brother is alive, or he does and has hid it from me. That thought triggers an onslaught of emotions and this time I empty the contents of my stomach into the toilet. With my eyes closed I rest my head on my forearm. My chest is heaving. I need to calm down before I hyperventilate. There's no way that Nate knew about Evan. He wouldn't do that to me or his mom and sister.

A soft knock brings me back from my thoughts. "I'll be out in a moment," I say, standing up and righting my dress. I hit the lever and move away. The mirror I stood in front of earlier offers me another glimpse of how bad I look, even more so now. My eyes are bloodshot and puffy. Turning the water on, I open the medicine cabinet to see if by chance she has toothpaste. I imagine she works long hours and maybe even spends the night on her couch. Not to mention she drinks coffee and doesn't want coffee-breath. Much to my relief, there's a tube. I quickly pull it out and squirt some onto my finger, brushing quickly and rinsing. With one last look in the mirror, I mutter to myself "this is as good as it's gonna get," before exiting.

The therapist is writing furiously across her pad of paper. The pad looks new and now I'm curious as to how many she's gone through today. I'm also wondering whether Evan and I are her most messed up case. Can't say anything I know about compares to what we're going through. I take the assumed position in the chair and wait for the next onslaught of questions.

"Feeling better?"

"Slightly," I say, nodding my assent. I'm not sure I'll ever feel one hundred percent, but I get up every day and put my pants on like any other normal person.

"Did you talk to any of the other wives or girlfriends from Evan's unit?"

"Mostly Frannie, she's River's wife. They had just gotten married a few days before the guys were called. We had been celebrating on the beach with a bonfire and a cookout. Kids were running around and some guys from different units and their families were there. That's the thing, the SEALs are a brotherhood and they're always going to protect their family.

"Anyway, we had been on the beach when the call came

in. River, he was their boss, got the call and just like that the atmosphere changed. The fire was extinguished and people started packing up and heading home to spend their last night with their loved ones. It's amazing how one phone call or a knock on the door can change everything.

"But to answer your question, Frannie and I hung out a lot. She's a little older than me, but she and River didn't have any children. She helped out a lot when EJ was born. Between her, Lois and my mom, I had someone at my house all the time."

"What about Evan and Nate's mom?"

I stand and walk over to the window. Evan is still sitting there, waiting for his turn.

"How much time do we have left?"

The therapist is quiet until I look at her. "Twenty minutes, but we can go over. I'm just seeing you and Evan today. We still have a lot to cover."

"What do you think you'll be able to tell us after all of this is over? This was Lois's idea, not mine, although I made Evan come. What are you going to do for us?" I look back at Evan and wish I were down there with him. I'm not sure what I'd say, but I think I'd like to hold his hand.

"Ryley, I'm hoping by the end of the day I can give you an assessment. Provide you with an outsider's opinion on which way you and Evan should go. It may not be what you're looking for but it may be exactly what you both need. We won't know that until we're done and I've had a chance to go over my notes."

I stand up straighter when I see a woman approach Evan. She's in NWU's, identical to his. He leans back and greets her as she sits down. I want to bang on the glass, but what good will it do me? I've moved on.

TWELVE

Evan

_____

I PONDER HER QUESTION. It would be so nice to talk to someone, anyone, who isn't tied to the military. All week I've been asking the questions, and each answer is *'it's classified'* or *'we don't have any recollection of that happening'*. My favorite one is, 'the mission went as planned.' No, the fuck it did. Snatch and grab and with a four man crew, I should've known something was up from the get-go.

However, I don't have the answers the doc is looking for. I only know what I know and what our mission was. If I tell her, is she at risk? Probably, but what if she's able to take my story and help Ryley and I figure out how to co-exist? As much as I'd love to think the doctor is going to convince Ry to stop her wedding, I don't think that's going to happen. Ryley owes me nothing, even if I think she does. She was the dutiful girlfriend waiting for my return, and when I didn't, she moved on. It's expected. She did exactly what I wanted her to do; I just didn't expect it to be with my brother.

"My unit leader, River, had just gotten married when we got the call. We had been home for some time, and I actually started to have a routine with Ryley. She'd get up with me in the morning, we'd make breakfast together and I'd make love to her before I left for work. I never wanted her to feel like we didn't have a last time together. I know it seems chauvinistic, but it was important to me that she and I had connected on that level before I went to base. Reporting to base each day, I never knew if I'd be home for dinner or not, so I had to treat each day like there wasn't a tomorrow morning.

"Anyway, we're at the beach, ya know? It's a normal day. The sun is out, we're eating and lots of guys and wives are there. River's phone rings, and he excuses himself. When he comes back, he says make sure everything is right at home. That was his code for we're leaving. Right then and there, everything shifted. It was time to go home, make everything right with our spouses and pack.

"River, Frannie, Ry and I were the last to leave, and as the girls walked to our cars, he stopped me and said that it was just four of us going: me, him, McCoy and Raskin. It wasn't the first time a unit of four had gone out, but the way River said it made me pause. We were heading into Cuba and a child of a U.S. politician had been kidnapped and taken there. Intel told us where the child was, and the commander said it'd be in and out.

"I echoed River's thought though and felt that something wasn't right. It wasn't our territory, and it should've been a unit from the east coast going, so why did we only have four members if we were going into hostile territory? He didn't have the answers and wasn't about to question our CO."

I stand and retreat to the water cooler and fill yet another paper cup. I keep my back to her, hiding my expression because this is harder than I thought. I shouldn't be talking about that day, but I feel like I'm left with no choice. The prize at the end of the tunnel, whether I win or not, is worth it.

"Had you ever felt this way about a mission previously?"

I shake my head. "Not even when we were in Afghanistan. We're elite. We've trained for everything possible. We may get nervous or excited, but it's not like we're jumping out of our skin. Jumping out of planes, walking through water and dense forest, it's second nature. This mission should've been easy compared to seeking shelter from a sand storm and being fired at by the Taliban."

I opt to sit on the couch instead of returning to the chair. Hopefully I can relax a little more now that the floodgates are open. I'm still mentally battling with the fact that someone has made a mistake. Mistakes cost people their lives and simply can't be made. Everything we do is checked and double-checked. We're efficient, perfectionists. At least I am.

"Some of my questions about while you were gone may seem out of the ordinary. I don't pretend to understand what it is that you do, and as I've stated, I'm here to help you and Ryley come to some sort of conclusion. The more we talk, the more it seems that there was a communication breakdown. Again," she says raising her hands. "I'm not in the service, I don't know. I'm simply making a guess on how four highly trained Navy SEALs disappeared, to have their families mourn their loss, only for you to return completely unaware that anything was amiss."

"You and me both," I mumble. She's right. Now that I sit here, too much of the past six years isn't adding up. If this is an error, it's a grave one, and someone had to know we'd return unless we weren't supposed to return. My time in Cuba is fresh. The memories are there. I have no doubt that McCoy, River or Raskin can recall every order, every maneuver we made to secure not only the child in question, but the many that we found when we arrived.

"When we found the missing child, we stumbled upon something bigger. We extracted the child and met at our rendezvous point. That was planned. What wasn't planned was the directive to go back to the site and…" I trail off, uncertain of what words could describe what we were told. I shrug and continue, "Secure the location. We were told that another unit was deploying immediately. We didn't think anything of it, until we got back to where the child was being held and everyone was gone."

The doc flips the page of her notepad and continues to write. I want to get up and take it from her hand and make sure she's not writing down something she shouldn't be. I know I have to trust that what she's writing is going to help Ryley and me, but with everything that has happened, it's hard for me to trust anything right now. It makes me wonder what's going through her mind.

"What happened next?"

"We started searching for clues as to the whereabouts of the missing, which took us deeper into the jungle. We lost our communications for a bit, but assumed command was aware of that. It was probably weeks, if not a month before we finally reached an elevation where we could use our Sat phone, but the orders were the same. Find the package and retrieve it. We reiterated that the package had been delivered, but the communications back were that it hadn't and to find it."

"At any time were you able to communicate with Ryley?"

My head shakes back and forth, my lips forming into a thin line. "Without sounding heartless, no I didn't. I'm there to do a job. I'm there to protect you and her from people who are trying to do our country harm. I'm not thinking about calling her to check in. I'm thinking about keeping my men alive. We're on a mission with a goal in sight. We stayed hidden, kept tracking the people we were looking for and checked in every few days with command."

"Did anyone ever come for you?"

"Yes, they brought us supplies, a new radio and they made sure our ammo was stocked. That's why this is so hard to understand. They had pictures of my son, letters from Ryley and my mom. But according to that newspaper article you showed me, I died months after being gone. None of this adds up. The Navy was supporting us, we were on a mission to recover children who were being used as sex slaves and someone here was telling everyone that we're dead!"

I stand and start pacing, stopping at the wall. My fist pounds against the wall, once, twice before I push away and run my hand over what little hair I have.

"Someone did some serious covering up, and it's costing me my life."

THIRTEEN

Ryley

"LET'S SHIFT A LITTLE and talk about your parents. Both your parents are in the military, right?"

I lean my elbow on the armrest of the couch. "My dad is a consultant for the Army Corps of Engineers, a federal employee. My mom is still active; she's stationed in Coronado. She takes EJ to work with her every now and again. EJ loves it. He wants to be like his grandma and his dad. I have no doubt that someday he'll wear the same uniform, but I've told you that already."

"I know, just going over my notes."

"Okay," I say meekly. My voice is tired. I'm tired. My session needs to be over.

"You met the Archers in Washington?"

I nod. "We did, but when Evan received his orders for Coronado, I applied to school in San Diego. Everyone thought I was stupid, but I wanted to be near him. My dad was livid and insisted that I apply everywhere so I could live my life and not worry about Evan or cater to his whereabouts. My mom encouraged me to enlist or become a lawyer like her, saying I might help someone one day like she does, but that's not what I wanted. It's not how I saw my life."

"How did you see your life?"

"With Evan, as his wife, raising our children while he's protecting our country. It was important to me that I support him and be there for him. I think it was important to him, as well, that he knew I'd be his support all the time, regardless of the situation."

"What if you were to break up?"

I shrug. "I tried to never think like that. I wanted to always be positive for Evan. Happy and welcoming. He was under enough stress that he didn't need mine as well."

"How many schools did you apply to?"

"Five, maybe? I don't remember. I wanted something close and really liked the area when I visited the schools there. When I was accepted at San Diego State I thought my dad was going to freak and refuse to pay for school. My mom though, she requested a transfer. They moved to Coronado about three months after I left for school."

"How did you feel having them so close?"

"Honestly, I didn't mind. I'm family orientated, so having them literally in my backyard was a blessing. I could drive home on the weekends and for holidays. I could've even lived at home, but being on campus gave Evan plenty of opportunities to spend the night. Having them there made it easy for me to make decisions. I didn't have to apologize to them because I was going to be spending the holidays with Evan. We were all together."

"And what about Evan's mom and sister? Where were they?"

"Julianne and Livvie stayed until the twins received their orders. Right now, they live in Sacramento."

"And all the parents get along?"

"Oh, I don't know about that." I hate that they don't, but there's nothing I can do about it. Our relationship is strained. "At first, yes, everyone got along and even more so after

Archie died, but since Evan… the tension started at his funeral. Like I said before, Julianne wanted things a certain way but Nate made sure I was afforded liberties. She was mad at Nate for a while, but eventually forgave him. Julianne questioned Evan's death and asked my mom to look into it. She wanted answers, and the Navy wasn't giving them to her. She expected my mom to find them out and my mom couldn't.

"I hadn't told anyone I was pregnant except for Evan and Nate so when I announced that I was… I don't know. Julianne didn't seem excited. I thought for sure she'd be thrilled, her son's legacy was going to live on and she'd still have a piece of Evan with her. At first she ignored the idea and that upset my father greatly. He couldn't understand how, after losing her husband and son, she wouldn't embrace my pregnancy.

"As I started to show and the more Nate brought me to her house, she came around. I know she was hurting, but so was I. I was trying to sustain a healthy pregnancy and bring Evan's child into this world when most of the time I wanted to curl up and be left alone.

"I can't imagine what's going to happen when Julianne finds out about Evan now."

The therapist leans forward as if she's intrigued in my soap opera life. "She doesn't know?"

I shake my head. "No, I don't believe she does. He… Evan said he wasn't ready to see her yet."

"And do your parents know?"

"Yes, they do. I called my mom because… because this whole situation seems so wrong and unrealistic. I need her to get answers."

Her hand moves fast over her sheet of paper. I can only imagine what she's putting down. *This family needs help!!!! This woman is bat-shit crazy.* I'm sure the list will be endless and I'll never get out of here. I have no doubt that I'll leave here with an itinerary of extensive therapy not for only me, but also for my family.

"How did your parents react to the news that Evan had died?"

"My dad was hurt. I've only seen him cry a few times in my life. I called him first because I needed him. He came right over, and I didn't even have to tell him. He just knew. He held me while I sobbed in his arms. He knew what it felt like, he's lost friends before, but this time it was like losing his son.

"He had once said to me that he didn't want me to marry into the military because he wanted me to experience a different life, but he understood that you can't help who you fall in love with. I didn't look at it as a military to non-military issue, I was in love with Evan and this was his job. I accepted that and was proud of him.

"My parents were proud of him too, and they let him know all the time. Evan's death hit them hard. Their daughter didn't just lose her fiancé, they also lost a son. My dad may have been a hard ass and strict, but he had respect for the twins and was especially close to Evan."

"A lot of family time, I'm gathering?"

"All the time, at least when Evan was home. Sunday dinners and weekend picnics were the norm. If Evan was just returning, my mom threw a big party for him. We'd all be together, Nate, Julianne and Livvie included. My parents made them feel welcomed and my mom even tried to set up Julianne with an officer from base, but she wasn't having it. She said that she wasn't lonely while she was still raising a teenage daughter."

"You mentioned earlier that things are strained with you and Julianne?"

"Yes, ever since Evan's funeral. I had hoped that things would change when EJ was born, but they didn't. Well, it did for EJ, but not for me. Julianne is close with EJ, and she tolerates me as his mother. I think that I'm a reminder or something. When Nate decided to reenlist, she berated me something fierce. She told me that I was taking her last son away from her. Sometimes I think she says things to EJ to make him question Nate's uniform."

"How is your mom with EJ?"

"Oh, EJ is her world. Since moving to California my dad fishes a lot, and when EJ was little, he kept him during the day and they'd do manly things, but my mom would take him on the weekends. They do everything together. She's taught him how to garden and make jam. They'll go apple picking in the fall, and she'll take him on base to show him off. He has his own set of NWU's that he wears proudly. EJ is grandma's angel. I know she wants more grandchildren and thought that Nate and I would expand our family, but now... well, now I'm not so sure that's going to happen."

"How do your parents feel about Nate?"

"My dad isn't as close to Nate as he was to Evan, but he still treats him fairly. They've been to sporting events, fishing trips, father-son stuff, but it's not the same, and Nate knows that. I think my dad doesn't want to get close. Fear has set in that one day Nate may not come back from a mission and we'll all be broken-hearted again. I'm not sure how many people you have to lose before you stop caring, but I think my dad is there at least. I could be there too."

"And your mother?"

"She's impartial. She wants to see me happy. She wants EJ to grow up with a strong family background. They're not joking when they say it takes a village to raise a child because it does, especially when you feel broken and beaten down. I depend a lot on my mom, not only to teach me, but to guide me into motherhood. I'm not sure how single parents do it. I commend them though. I have a whole army of people ready and willing on a moment's notice to drop what they're doing to help me."

"Army?" she questions with a raised eyebrow.

For the first time I can feel myself smile. "Bad pun, sorry," I say, jokingly. Maybe this will help, but then again maybe not. A little glimmer of hope can go a long way though.

FOURTEEN

Evan

"LET'S TALK ABOUT YOUR return home."

I scoff and pull the chair away from her desk, harder than I wanted, but it earns me an inquisitive look. This is another subject I don't want to talk about. The most anticipated return home turning into the most epic failure of all.

"Really not something I want to talk about."

She folds her hands, much like the principal used to do when I had to report to his office. This is their "calm" look. She's calmly going to tell me this is for my own good and that the sooner we get this out in the open the sooner we can – or I can – move on. Ryley apparently didn't have any problems moving on.

"We landed; no one was there to greet us. I got a cab ride home. End of story."

The doctor leans back in her chair, rocking slightly before sighing. "I know this has to be the hardest question for you, Evan. Just remember the goal."

I close my eyes and shake my head. Never in the years that I've been in combat did I experience something so heart-breaking and demoralizing as the day we came home.

"It was raining when we landed. As soon as the C-130

touched down, we were out of our jump seats before the engine was shut off. Coming home from deployment is sometimes met with little to no fanfare. There are times when we get the job done, and bam, we're right back home and in time for dinner. Other times, the wives, girlfriends and kids are there with their banners and balloons.

"When my unit returned from Afghanistan, the welcoming party was top notch. The San Diego State marching band was there. Speeches were given. We had refreshments, the whole nine-yards. What people don't realize is that while the party is nice, we just want to be home. We want to acclimate to our surroundings. We want to kiss our women good and proper. We want to scratch our balls without the TV cameras watching us.

"Anyway, when we stepped off, nothing. Our CO had been on the bird with us and he literally patted us on the back and said *'see you at 0800 for debriefing.'* We watched, dumbfounded, as he got into a car and drove off. He just left us there. It's a pretty shitty feeling returning home after being gone for six years to find no one waiting for you and your CO not care how you were getting back home."

"What'd you do?"

"Stood there, scratching our heads, wondering why there were taxis waiting for us."

"Did you find it odd that your..." she pauses and looks over her notes. "Your CO, as you call him, left you there?"

"At the time, it didn't really cross my mind. I was too excited to be back home."

"Any strange looks from when you were on base?"

Now that I'm sitting here, and she's brought up the idea that maybe the Navy is responsible, her question makes all the sense in the world.

"That's another thing," I add, "that strikes me as odd. We were dropped off on an empty airfield with taxis waiting to take us back to base. No one was there to collect our weapons.

We had a full arsenal, and we were in the middle of nowhere. I felt like we were in a ghost town."

"In hindsight, you were the ghost," she says quietly.

"Apparently so," I answer quietly. It's a hard pill to swallow knowing that your family and friends thought you died. They mourned you, they moved on the whole time you're fighting to free children from sex trafficking.

"And when you saw Ryley?"

"I need a break," I say quickly before standing. "I need..."

"It's okay, Evan. The bathroom is right there." She points to the door adjacent to her office. My strides are long, with my steps pounding into the carpet. I open the door and step into the bathroom. It's small and confined, but perfect for a one-person office. I lean my head against the tiles and bask in their coolness. I didn't feel flush out in the room, but I definitely do now. I want to understand how everything became so screwed up. Who dropped the ball and why? Why weren't more units dispatched and why were we sent to an east coast territory? None of this is adding up or making sense. River was correct to have doubts. We should've expressed them before we left, but we didn't. We accepted our orders, assumed our brothers on the other units were tied up and went to do our jobs.

This doctor shows me doubt, and I hate that. I've never questioned the Navy or my job. I'm proud of what I do, but now I'm second-guessing this mission and why it took so long with the extraction. We went for one package that we sealed and delivered. We should've been on that chopper heading back with it. Instead, we were picking up the pieces of destroyed lives and for what? That's what I want to know. How could someone do this to us?

When I come out, the doc is watering her plants. She looks at me and smiles reassuringly as she puts down the pitcher and takes a seat.

"Are you ready to continue?"

I nod, even though I'm more eager to beat my feet back to the base and find out what the hell is going on. I need to find Raskin, too. I haven't seen him since we returned and he has to know something's up. Did he have a bunk ready? Was there any preparation? Come to think of it, I haven't seen my CO all week either. River, McCoy, Raskin and I need to put our heads together and figure this shit out.

"Are we almost done?" I ask, looking at the clock before she can answer me. It seems that time has come to a complete standstill, the big hand barely ticking off the minutes. I'm emotionally drained. I have been all week, but today is really taking it all out of me.

"You were going to tell me what happened when you saw Ryley for the first time."

"Right," I mumble as I think back to where I left off. "Um… yeah so we took a cab. River and McCoy don't live far from us so they got out first. When the driver pulled up, I peered out the window, looking at the two-story home that we bought together and thought, 'wow, she's done an amazing job,' not that I didn't think she would, because Ryley is beyond amazing. She makes it… or made it easy to be a SEAL. Her support has always been unwavering, very solid. Again, it didn't escape my notice that, again, the banners were missing. No 'Welcome Home' sign and the lack of people confused me.

"Of course, I didn't have my keys so I had to sit on the swing and wait. Funny thing is, now that I'm sitting here talking about it, it didn't occur to me that River and McCoy were lacking the same fanfare. The only thing on my mind in that moment was seeing Ry and meeting my son. I knew the pictures I had been receiving didn't do him justice, and I wanted to hold him."

"I'm sorry, Evan, I don't mean to interrupt, but did you say pictures?"

"Yeah, each time we'd meet at a rendezvous for supplies

and to extract more children, we'd get care packages, letters and photos from home. McCoy and I are the only ones with kids and that had to be the worst thing, watching our children grow up in photos. But now that I'm saying it out loud, I know that those packages didn't come from Ryley. None of it makes sense."

The doc shakes her head slowly and scribbles across her notepad. "Evan, I hope that you see there is something very mysterious about your deployment."

"I'm starting to, yes."

"Please continue." Her hand moves in a circular motion as she speaks.

"Ryley pulled up and got out of her car with a bag of groceries in her hand. I stood and watched her as she realized that someone was on the porch. She looked at me, her expression unreadable. The bag dropped, and my reflex was to catch it. I flew down the stairs, and she gasped, stopping me dead in my tracks. I smiled, and it felt like the first day I met her all over again... until it didn't.

"'*Hey, Ry.*'" My voice cracked, ya know because I hadn't seen her in so long. "'*I'm home.*'" It was when I reached for her that I knew something was wrong. Her eyes filled instantly with tears, and I thought, why isn't she jumping into my arms? Why isn't she kissing me all over?"

"'*Who... what...?*'" She started shaking her head, and I tried to step forward, but she held her hand up. "'*Don't, please don't.*'"

"'*I don't understand, Ryley. I know I've been gone a long time, but I'm home now.*'"

"'*No, you don't understand. You're dead to us... to me... who...? How are you here right now?*'"

"Her words threw me back ten steps. I hadn't a clue what she was talking about, and she kept repeating over and over again that I was dead and not supposed to be there. I stood in the yard, watching her fall apart but she wouldn't let me help her. She wouldn't let me touch her.

"It's when she started wiping her eyes that I saw her ring. It wasn't the one I had bought, the one that I had saved a year for. This one was different. I knew then that she had given herself to someone else."

"*'Why?'*" I asked her, repeatedly. My voice was something I hadn't recognized since my dad passed away. It only took an instant for my world to crash down around me, for my heart to drop to the ground leaving me open to every imaginable pain possible. For the first time in a long time I was crying and she was standing there matching me tear for tear.

"I asked her again, why, and she shook her head. "*'You're dead. How is this... why?'*" But I didn't want to hear those words from her. "*'Who?'*" I asked her next, and she dropped her head, covering her face with her hands. I couldn't wait any longer for her answer so I went to her, grasping her wrists in my hand and pulling them away from her face. "*'Who gave you that ring, Ryley?'*"

"*'Nate. I'm marrying Nate because you're dead. You've been dead for so long. So long... why are you doing this to me?'*"

"I stepped back, dropping her hands. It was like her words burned me. They did in a way."

"*'I'm not dead, Ryley. Why would you think that?'*"

"*'We buried you. We had a funeral, and you were put into the ground with honors. Other SEALs were there. Their Tridents are imbedded in your casket. How are you standing in front of me? Are you real? Are you really my Evan because I cried on your grave for months and months, and now you're standing in front of me like nothing is wrong?'*"

"*'Of course I am. I don't know what you're saying here, Ry. What's going on?'*"

"Her head was shaking back and forth. She was shaking, and the tears were breaking my heart. We were standing in the driveway, and it dawned on me that she was alone."

"'Where's my son?'"

"'How… How do you even know I had a boy?'"

"'I've seen the pictures, Ry.'"

"Her head popped up so fast I thought it was going to fall off her shoulders. She told me he was in daycare, said that his name was EJ and that he was named after me; I told her that I knew that already. Thing is, I knew everything… well, almost everything. They did fail to mention that my fiancé had moved on though. Between her confusion and the lack of fanfare, I knew something was up, I just didn't know the extent."

I fist my hands into my eyes and wipe angrily at the tears. Her hand presses down on my shoulder softly, and when I pull away there's a box of tissue waiting for me. "Thanks," I mumble, taking a few from the box and covering my face. I've tried not to think about this day since it happened, and I know it's necessary to talk about, but it's painful. Everything about this past week has been nothing but anger and pain.

FIFTEEN

Ryley

"DO YOU WANT TO talk about EJ?" she asks. Normally I'd respond with a resounding yes, but right now the answer is no. I feel like I've failed my little boy in every way possible. I don't know how I'm going to sit him down and tell him that Evan is his dad and that Nate is just playing daddy so that he didn't feel left out at school. We should've corrected him when he first called Nate daddy, but we didn't. We thought this would be a good thing for EJ. We thought giving him a father figure would help ease the pain when he was older and we told him about Evan.

That was our plan from the beginning. We'd sit EJ down when he was older, when he could better understand, and tell him about Evan. Show him pictures of his dad. Tell him stories about how he's a hero and how proud EJ should be to be named after him. EJ would understand then, but now? Now he'll be confused and hurt, and it's my fault.

"What do you want to know?" I ask, leaving the door open for anything. It's not going to matter what she asks. Everything I tell her about EJ will tear me wide open.

"How old is he?"

"He's five. He'll start kindergarten in the fall."

"Is he excited?"

"He is." I do something I least expect of myself by pulling out my wallet and showing her a picture of him. He's standing next to my dad and mom wearing NWU's like my mom. EJ's red hair looks shaggy under this cap, but he stands there next to my dad proud to be his mini-me.

"He's adorable."

"Thanks," I say, tucking my wallet back into my purse. "He looks just like Evan. At least I think he does. My mom says he looks like me, but aside from his hair color, he's all Evan. He acts just like him."

"I find that surprising considering Nate raised him. You mentioned earlier that the twins are the opposite of each other."

"I do too. Nate is so calm about everything, whereas Evan was wild. EJ is wild and sometimes out of control, at least for me, but he's nothing like Nate. EJ wants all the excitement and the reward. He knows if he sets his mind to something the payoff will be there at the end. Even at five, he knows about hard work."

"Are you afraid he'll go into the service?"

"No. I know I should be considering… but I'm not. It's in his blood. I think I'd be more shocked if he didn't enlist at eighteen."

The therapist shifts the papers on her desk before leaning back in her chair. "You have a big task on your hands where your son is concerned."

"I know," I say, honestly. It's the one thing that I do know. I don't care if he's five or fifteen. He's not going to under-stand that his dad is Evan, and when he asks why, what do I say? *I'm sorry, we were told he was dead,* and expect everything to be okay? I can't even wrap my head around that at the moment; how's he supposed to?

"Well, that's one of the reasons you're here today. So let me help you. The first thing I'm going to tell you is that it's not going to matter how you say it, it'll sound wrong to you because of the pain you're in. You need to understand that your son is resilient. Yes, he won't understand at first—"

"I don't understand. How am I supposed to explain it to my son? He... he loves Nate and I can't tell Nate to go away, but I also can't tell Nate to stay because Evan deserves a chance to get to know his son. And EJ... he deserves them both.

"God, I'm so confused and frustrated," I say, standing up. "I don't know what to do, and you don't have the answer. Sitting EJ down is the only answer, but he's not going to understand it. He's not going to comprehend his mommy sitting him down and showing him a picture of Evan and saying hey *bud, sorry, Nate really isn't your dad, but this guy is*. In this fantasy world I've been living in, none of this happens, and I'm getting married soon. We healed. He died. We buried him. We said our goodbyes and moved on."

I stand with my back to her, afraid that she'll cringe at the way I look right now. I must look like an evil witch to her, but I can't help it. I just want some happy in my life, and I thought I was getting that. I thought I had earned it.

"The day Evan's mom showed up at our house asking for his flag, I told her I was pregnant. I asked her if she really wanted to take Evan's legacy away from his son. She sat there, stoically, with her hands holding a picture of Evan. The picture, just a random one that I had out, was from his basic training."

"'Where did you get this?'"

"'Evan. He sent it to me when he was in basic.'"

"'He gave you everything, didn't he?'"

"'We're engaged, Julianne, why wouldn't he share everything with me?'"

"'Were.'"

"'What?'"

"'You were engaged.'"

"'Julianne, I'm still having his son. We created this child together, and he knew he was having a child before he…'"

"'You can say it.'"

"'No, I can't.'"

"I never understood how she could talk about Evan being gone so quickly. I couldn't. Even when he was deployed, I acted like he was coming home any day just so I had peace of mind. I can't imagine what she went through when she lost her husband and again to lose her son, but I wasn't her enemy.

"My pregnancy was without complications. Whenever Nate was home he was making sure I was eating. Lois or Frannie, she's River's wife, were at all my appointments, and Carter helped Nate build EJ's crib. Lois, she did this amazing collage of Evan, which is EJ's wallpaper. So many people gave me photos after Evan died that she took them and had them made into wallpaper. Still to this day, EJ's room is my favorite room in the house.

"I was alone when I delivered. I told my mom that if Evan couldn't be with me, no one could. So I did it by myself. There was no one to hold my hand or tell me to push just a little bit harder. I felt Evan with me though. I knew he was in the room. But knowing what I know now, it was just a figment of my imagination. He could've been there when his son was born, but he wasn't. When I think back to that day…" I shake my head to clear my thoughts. "I gave birth to EJ alone. I was empty inside and sobbed when the nurse set him on my chest. Evan wasn't there to share that moment with me. I held our son and cried until there was nothing left. I wasn't happy after I had EJ because everything was different. I was alone. I was left alone, and nothing can change that."

"You're not alone now, though, Ryley."

I scoff. "I guess that depends on your definition of alone."

"Do you think Evan feels alone?"

I bite my lower lip, likely drawing blood, to keep myself from crying. Only my self-inflicted pain doesn't stop the tears from flowing.

"I know Evan feels like he's alone. It's hard to describe, but I've always felt connected to him. Even when they told me he died, it was hard to believe. I thought that I'd feel my heart stop when he died, that I would know, but it was nothing like that. I had always sensed him around me, or would imagine him walking into the room I was in, and seconds later, there he was. I tried to explain myself to him once, and all he did was nod and say he felt it too.

"I should've trusted my instincts, but I'm supposed to trust the people he works for and I did, and now look at where we are – sitting in your office trying to come up with a decent resolution."

"Why do you call the resolution decent, Ryley?" she asks, sliding her notepad to the side of her desk. I find it hard to believe she's done analyzing my life, but I'm willing to appease her.

"Like I've said, there's so much hurt in my family right now, decent would be a godsend. Regardless of any choice I make, brothers will be torn apart. A family that has healed is once again experiencing the wounds that destroyed all of us. Julianne doesn't know her son is alive, and Nate doesn't know about his brother. Regardless of what Evan says, Nate wouldn't hide this from me."

"What did Evan say?"

I reach for a tissue and dab at my eyes. Today can't end fast enough for me. "The day that Evan returned and I told him about Nate, Evan kept saying Nate knew. Everything from that day is so confusing. I didn't ask Evan to elaborate. I didn't think I needed to. I was in shock."

"You don't sound so sure," she states, adding to my uncertainty.

"That's because I'm not. Seeing him standing there, none of it makes sense."

The therapist picks up her pad and when I think she's about to write another novel about my life, she slides it into an open desk drawer. She places her folded hands on top of her desk and attempts to smile. I know it's hard for her to listen to my sob story and not judge me. I'm thankful she did.

"As you know, I'm going to meet with Evan in a little while, but we're not done. I'm very aware of your timeline to get things resolved. If I were in your shoes, I'd postpone the wedding until the three of you can sort everything out. I'm not saying cancel, but just put it off for a bit. I'm afraid you'd do yourself and Nate an injustice if you went through with the ceremony as planned.

"I've cleared my calendar this week and plan to see you and Evan – together – in the next couple of days to discuss what methods need to be implemented for both of you to be successful parents to EJ because frankly, he's the most important person in this travesty and we need to make sure he's well taken care of."

I nod and stand, extending my hand to her. "I'm sorry I was so rude and absent when we began. I've had years of talking about Evan, to find closure and to have those wounds ripped open – sitting down and talking to a stranger was not something I wanted to do."

"I completely understand, Ryley." She stands and walks me to the door. I pause, with my hand on the knob and brace myself. Evan could be there, waiting. We could see each other, make eye contact and both would see how much hurt we've been going through. Only, I don't sense him there, but I've learned not to follow my gut anymore.

"He's not there, Ryley, if that's why you're waiting." I let her words linger in the air as I open the door slowly to find Lois still with her nose in a magazine, just like I left her. She looks up, smiles softly and stands to take my hand.

SIXTEEN

Evan

"EVAN, I THINK WE'RE finished for today."

My head lifts quickly as I meet her gaze. There is a look of pity masking her smile. She can pity me. It's understandable. If I were in her shoes I'd pity the person I am right now. I chance a look at the clock and see that I still have a few more minutes. Maybe she feels how broken I am and needs time to regroup or find someone else to fix me.

"Okay," I say hesitantly. I'm not sure I want to go through this again with another doctor, and definitely not a military one.

The doc folds the page of her notepad over and slides it into her desk. She smiles softly. "I'm going to tell you the same thing I told Ryley this morning. My schedule has been cleared this week so I can help get things resolved, or heading toward a resolution. My plan is to see you and Ryley together in the next couple of days to discuss what methods need to be implemented for both of you. My concern is EJ. You need to be able to bond with him and she understands that."

She stands, coming over to me. "My suggestion, and I didn't tell this to Ryley, is for you to spend some time with her. She's hurting, Evan. While you thought everything was fine, aside from the fact that you were gone for so long, she buried you and tried to move on with her life. She's making neither heads nor tails of what's happening right now, but give her time without letting her slip through the cracks."

My body sighs as I stand, as if it knows I don't have to sit in that chair anymore. My feet shuffle toward the door, leaving the doc leaning up against her desk. "Thank you," I say before opening the door and leaving the room.

The sun is bright and penetrating when I step out of the office. I have to shield my eyes quickly before I walk out into traffic. Once my eyes adjust, I look across the street to the park hoping to see Ryley sitting over there. If she were, it'd be so much easier to talk to her right now, although the thought of bringing her to base makes more sense to me since she wouldn't be able to run away from me. Somehow, however, I don't think Ryley wants to be anywhere near the base – not that I can blame her. At this point, I don't want to be there either, except it's the only choice I have since I'm not really welcome in my own home.

With only one other destination in mind, I text the guys and ask them to meet me. We need to figure out what's going on. Each of our situations is different, yet we're all experiencing the same thing. I also need to bite the bullet and call my mother. I'm not sure why I haven't yet. I guess I've been waiting to see if our unearthly return would make the news, but so far nothing has been reported. Every time I learn another factoid about this deployment, I'm more convinced that it was not legit.

Pulling in front of Magoo's, it would be easy to go drown my sorrows in beer, but I need to keep a level head about the situation. If I ask the wrong person a question, who knows what could happen? As is, someone high up has taken away my life. It doesn't matter that I'm standing here today or not. I'm not the same person and someone needs to pay.

It's a happy relief to walk in and be surrounded by

friends. The bar stools are full of patrons, men I've served with in the past. Tables are thrown together to make bigger spaces and the same chairs are still here. An American flag hangs on the wall with various pictures surrounding it. All these pictures have been given or sent to Rick, the owner, for display. I refuse to look at the wall that holds all our past SEALs. I know the four of us are up there or maybe Rick has taken them down. Either way, I'm not looking, at least not today.

I've spent many hours trying to figure out what happened and answering all the questions I could. It's very unsettling to know that people thought you were dead.

It only takes me a second or two to spot Raskin and McCoy.

Justin "Rask" Raskin, being the single guy he is, only had to deal with his parents on his return. His mom fainted after she answered the phone and his dad threatened to beat whoever was on the other end. They're arriving tomorrow. We've all promised to be there for him when he sees them for the first time. I think that's another reason why I can't call my mom. I need to see her and Livvie, and I know I can't continue to put it off any longer. Thing is, spending time with my son and his mother is more important. Well, his mother is the icing on my unfrosted cake. If I get any time with her it'll be worth it.

Tucker McCoy is our sniper and a damn good one. When we met back at the base after our fateful return, his story was similar to mine except his wife left and took their daughter. She didn't leave a forwarding address and isn't in her home-town. How he knows the latter is beyond me. I'm not going to ask. In fact, I try not to ask any questions because our wounds are so deep it's like pouring salt in them, rinsing and repeating.

The guys are sitting at the table throwing the beers back. I can't help but wonder if they were already here when I called them. I probably would've been had I not agreed to the therapy session today.

Just as I sit down, Raymond "River" Riveria, walks in. He receives pats on the back, shares handshakes and is admired by our fellow brothers. He's our fire team leader and a damn fine one at that. Frannie, his wife, and Ryley are friends; at least, they were when we left. River's the lucky bastard of the group. His wife welcomed him home with open arms and then vowed vengeance on whoever is responsible for the colossal fuck-up. Frannie offered their extra bedroom to me, but I declined. They haven't seen each other in years, the last thing they need is a roommate. River and Frannie also know everything about what's going with Ryley. It's a bit comforting to hear from Frannie that Nate and Ryley didn't just fall in love and that she refused him for years, even though it still hurts and doesn't really change my opinion of the situation.

Since our return, it's been a never-ending cycle of pain. I'm starting to wonder if we were better off never coming back. Most of the wives and families had accepted that we were dead, and yet here we are ripping open healed wounds without any of the answers that our families and we need so desperately.

There's an uncomfortable silence at the table. It's completely different from when you're meeting someone for the first time and you've run out of things to talk about. This silence is deafening, scary. We have too much to say with far too many questions to ask, and we're all afraid of the answers.

A fresh pitcher of beer is set on the table and two other glasses added. I nod at Slick Rick, who is a dear friend of all the SEALs. He's owned this bar for years and has always catered to the Navy. As far as he's concerned this is our establishment. He's open seven days a week and when I asked him why, he said the military is always working and so was he. As soon as our glasses are filled, we raise them toward the bar, acknowledging our thanks. Rick waves us off as if thanks aren't needed.

"I'm hiring a private investigator." It's McCoy who breaks the silence. He's lost the most out of our group. While some may think that he's in the same boat I am, it's not strictly true. I have the luxury of seeing Ryley whenever I want even if it tears me apart. McCoy hasn't seen his daughter, who was three when we left, and now she's gone.

"It's smart," River says, as he sits down. "Frannie wants us to talk to someone from the CIA to help us."

"Why?" Rask asks, which honestly dumfounds me.

"Because something happened to us and our families," I say. "After the shit I learned today, the articles I read... this mission we were on was a cover-up for something bigger and we were pawns." I chug down my glass of beer and refill it, emptying the pitcher. No sooner do I set it down, another one appears. Rick just knows.

"I know someone, or at least I did, in the CIA," I add. "Her name is Cara, and she used to date my brother." Before my mission, I left thinking that Nate and Cara would be headed toward the altar and may even beat Ryley and me. Now I think his relationship with her was just a front to hide his feelings toward Ryley. "I'll have to tread lightly where she's concerned though. I don't know how she and Nate ended."

The guys all nod in agreement as we delve right back into the uncomfortable silence. That seems to be our norm. We sit and think about the shit storm our lives have become. There isn't a real use in talking about it because we don't have answers.

Before long, Frannie is at our table. She sits next to me, offering me comfort. The talk turns to sports and the weather. We don't say much in front of Frannie, but we know that River has been talking to her. I'd be doing the same thing if I had Ryley. Never have I felt the need to talk about a mission before. I'd never break my oath, but I have a feeling if I don't talk about it or write it down, facts are going to get lost or forgotten. I, for one, can't afford to forget anything.

"Dinner tomorrow night at our house," Frannie announces with such enthusiasm that McCoy and Rask agree immediately. "We'll barbeque and maybe get a little surfing in if the waves are good and with Rask's parents arriving, it will be a nice neutral ground."

"Sounds good," I say, even though she knows I'll be there regardless. I don't have any other place to go and staying on base right now is bringing me down.

It doesn't take long for McCoy to leave. He has business to tend to and he won't say anything in front of Frannie. Rask follows shortly after, stating that with his parents arriving, he needs some sleep. We know that's not true, but we're not about to argue.

"Ryley Clarke, I haven't seen you in here in a long time. Glad to see you, sweetheart." My head pops up at Rick's voice calling out Ryley's name. This is the first time I've seen her in here since we came back, and the fact that she's only a few feet away from me causes my heart to go into palpations. I finish off my beer and am about to pour another glass when Frannie stops me.

"Keep your wits about you, Archer. Maybe she's here to talk. I can tell you that once we got the news she stopped coming here, so this is a big step for her."

Frannie's confession throws me for a six. She just confirmed what I've been meaning to ask her all week – she and Ryley stayed in contact. My elation of that fact quickly dissipates when I realize that Frannie would have also known about Nate.

I set down my glass to appease Frannie's suggestion. The last thing I want is to make Ryley uncomfortable or be too intoxicated if I speak to her, because I'm really hoping that, by the way she's staring at me, she intends to come over.

My hopes are quickly met when she heads in our direction. Frannie stands and greets her with a long hug. I'm jealous, but grateful that they have each other. Ryley hugs River next and I know it's too much to hope that I'll get a hug, so I don't stand to greet her and that pains me.

I try not to look too shocked when the old wooden chair next to me is pulled out. The scraping on the ground as she scoots forward is what gets my attention. There are four other seats and she took the one next to me. I have to sit on my hand to keep myself from reaching out and touching her. The world is a cruel place right now. I can't be who I am with her because of the hand we've been dealt. As much as I love having her next to me, she has to remember that nothing has changed for me. It's taking every bit of will power that I have to not pull her into my side. Her body is angled toward me as if it knows that I'm slowly dying on the inside.

"Hi, it's really good to see you, River. Frannie you look so happy." Not only does she not say hi to me, she tells River it's good to see him. What am I? Chopped liver? Do I stink or something?

"Tomorrow night at our house, we're having a barbeque, you should come." If I could kiss Frannie, I would right now.

"That'd be great, but I think we're going to head to Sacramento."

Frannie nods, but Ryley's statement leaves me confused.

"What's in Sacramento?"

Ryley clears her throat and starts picking apart a paper napkin. "Your mom and Livvie still live there. I thought that we could take EJ up and stay for a night or two."

"What?" my voice cracks with desperation and excitement. This whole week I've only seen glimpses of my son and have yet to meet him. I understand Ryley's hesitation, but dammit if I don't want to hold my boy. As much as I need to see my mom and sister, I'd much rather take the time to get to know my son and figure out a way to get my girl back. I can always call my mom.

"Oh, Ryley, that's a wonderful idea." I look at Frannie, who's nodding and River who is looking at me. I chance a glance at Ryley and see that her eyes are damp with unshed tears.

Ryley meets my gaze and smiles. "I don't know what I'm going to tell EJ, Evan, but I'm going to do it tonight. I can't keep this bottled up any longer."

I nod slowly, unable to find my voice.

"Would you like me there?" Frannie asks, again making me feel better that she and Ryley remained friends.

"No," she says with a small smile. "I think I'll be okay."

I have to excuse myself immediately for fear of a colossal breakdown and something like that can't happen in Magoo's. River follows me, as I expected him to, into the men's room.

I clutch the sink and stare at my reflection in the decades-old mirror.

"Everything's going to be fine," River says, standing next to me.

"I'm nervous. What if he doesn't like me?"

He shakes his head. "From what I've learned, there's a mural of you in his room, something one of Ryley's friends did. Frannie has spoken so much about EJ and how great a kid he is, I think you're going to find out you have nothing to worry about."

"Except total rejection from my son."

River shakes his head. "Frannie tells me he's the spitting image of you."

I roll my eyes. "Great, that must drive Ryley crazy."

"There are worse things in life." He's right, too. He takes his leave and I follow soon after. I half expect Ryley to be gone when I return, but she's still sitting there chatting with Frannie. I use this moment to fully appraise her. Everything about her is the same as I remember, yet different. She's more refined. More woman and less girl. I hate that I missed all the changes she went through and even standing here and thinking about the days... years that I missed, I want to hurt someone.

Ryley glances up and catches me staring. I smile and turn away bashfully but keep my eyes on her. The draw I feel toward her is still there. She's pulling me by a string and before I know it, I'm sitting next to her again.

"What'd I miss?" I ask nonchalantly, acting as if this is the norm for us, the four of us sitting around a table and drinking beer while River and I discuss our workday – sans important details, of course.

"We were just talking about dinner," Ryley says, catching my eye.

"Yeah, the mess hall is definitely not on my list of places to visit tonight."

She shakes her head and takes a deep breath. "I thought maybe you'd come over in a half hour, have dinner with us. We can talk to EJ, together." Her voice is so small, but forceful. She has no idea that her words slice through my gut even though they're the most joyous words I've heard all week.

"You and EJ?" It's a dumb question, but I need confirmation that my brother isn't home yet. I'm not ready to see him.

"Yes, plus my parents. They missed you, and my dad wants to see you."

I bite the inside of my cheek to keep my emotions in check. I nod, unable to find the words to express how grateful I am right now. Her father, he stepped up after my dad died. He made me feel like a son and welcomed me into his family with open arms.

"I'd love to."

My car idles in front of the house Ryley and I used to share. The lawn is in need of cutting, and it makes me wonder if she does it or if she pays someone to come by. I suppose Nate takes care of it, but what if he's not here? Who helps her? Not that she needs help. Ryley is one of the most independent, fiercely loyal and dedicated people I know. Aside from my 'death,' I don't think there's anything she can't handle.

A knock on my window startles me. Ryley is bent over with her hands on her bare knees. She's no longer wearing a dress, but is now in cut-off jeans and a t-shirt. Her gorgeous, red hair is piled high in what she used to call her study bun. I press down on the lever, lowering my window. She crouches down, resting her arms where the window was.

"You okay?"

My eyes meet hers, making me smile. She doesn't have a clue what her words are doing to me today, but I need to find a way to tell her.

"I'm pretty nervous."

Ryley chuckles, and I smile again. It feels damn good to smile with a purpose. "Worse than first date nervous?"

"No, having a first date with you was the easiest thing I ever did." I run my hand down my leg. "I don't know how to answer some of the questions, or how I'm supposed to feel. They thought I was dead and I... "

"Listen, my parents love you, and they're concerned. You know Mom is going to start an investigation into this, and I can promise you that they won't talk about it tonight."

I nod and the question that has been plaguing me since earlier in the bar comes to mind. "Why are you doing this?"

Ryley moves away from my car slightly, before clearing her throat. "Today, in therapy, she reminded me that this isn't your fault. You didn't choose to be gone or have them tell us you're dead. You have a right to know EJ, just as he has a right to know his dad, but he thinks Nate is his dad, and I'm not sure how to tell him otherwise."

The sound of Nate's name being mentioned turns my insides, but I get it. I understand. At least, I think I do.

"I want to know my son, Ryley. I want to be his dad."

Tears glisten in her eyes. "I know, Evan. I want that too."

I look briefly at the house and pull the handle to open the door. Ryley backs away, allowing me to get out. We walk side by side for the first time in years back into our house, each step bringing me closer to the inevitable.

As soon as the door opens, laughter starts to fill the void in my heart. The living room is exactly the way I remember it, but now an American flag sits on top of the mantle next to my picture and my medals. A normal person would go over and look at them, but I don't care. They're tainted.

"I didn't change much after you... the couch is new, but the same. I had someone rebuild it for me because I couldn't part with it."

"It's just a couch, Ry."

She shrugs. "I know, but you loved it."

I follow the voices, leading me toward the backyard. I know what I'm going to find, and even though my head says I'm prepared, my heart isn't. I know Ryley's close, I can feel her. My hand rests on the handle of the sliding glass door. Ry's hand comes down on top of mine, and she gives it a little tug.

"He'll love you, Evan," she says as she pushes open the door.

We step out onto the deck, and the laughter stops. Her

mom spots me first and covers her mouth. I hate that she's about to cry. When her arms wrap around me, her words are soft in my ears. "I'm so sorry, Evan. So very sorry." I give her a squeeze and release her.

Her dad steps up to me and holds out his hand. A man of little emotion, it works for me. "You missed our fishing date." I nod, again biting the inside of my cheek.

"Sorry, sir. It won't happen again." A smile breaks out on his face as he pulls me into a hug. "Glad you're home, son."

"Me too." Jensen Clarke is a man of few words and emotions so when he pulls away and hides his face from my view, I know he's feeling the same as me. We've been cheated out of a lifetime of memories and for what, I don't know, but I'm going to find out.

Ryley comes into view walking up the steps from the back yard. She's holding the hand of my five-year-old son who isn't the spitting image of me, but of his mother. This time, there's no biting of the cheek because the tears are flowing freely down my face. EJ stands next to Ryley and stares at me. His eyes move all around as he takes me in. I crouch down to get a better look at him. EJ's blue eyes shine against his dark, red hair.

"I know you," he says, much to my surprise.

"Oh yeah?" I have to clear my throat to beat the frog that has taken up residence there.

"Yeah, you're on my walls."

I turn my attention to Ryley for confirmation, but her eyes are downcast. There's a small hint of a smile forming; she's trying to fight it. I've seen this look many times. She's embarrassed, but she shouldn't be. She was trying to preserve my memory. I get it. I just wish it never had to happen in the first place.

"I can't wait to see your room," I reply, hoping he understands that I want to see not only his bedroom, but also everything else he wants to show me.

"Mommy, is he the other Eban? You know the one I talk about in my prayers?"

I choke, and Carole sobs. Her hand quickly covers her mouth as Jensen pulls her into his arms. Ryley's a trooper though; she's holding it together perfectly. I, on the other hand, am shaking like a leaf.

"Yes, EJ, this is Evan." That's all she says, not that I'm expecting more but am hoping.

"That's my name, too!" he says with a smile complete with a missing front tooth. Before I can say anything, a long, wet nose, followed by a larger head is thrust between us. EJ is knocked down, but laughs. I stagger, catching myself before I hit the deck.

"Deefur, knock it off," EJ says, pushing his hair out of his face and standing back up. Deefur was just a pup when I bought him for Ryley. He's a black lab and was purchased with the intent to train. I wanted Ryley to feel safe when I was gone. He was supposed to be the answer, not my brother.

"Dat's my dog," EJ giggles.

"I remember him when he was a puppy."

"He's really big now. Do you wanna see my room?"

Leave it to the five year old to change the subject and bring me back to the here and now.

SEVENTEEN

Ryley

THERE ARE MOMENTS IN my life that I have imagined: Evan holding my hand when I gave birth to EJ, meeting him at the end of the aisle, watching our son grow. Some of them I think of over and over again, but nothing could ever prepare me for seeing Evan and EJ standing side by side. When I was pregnant, I had to pretend that Evan's hands were wrapped around me, cradling our child, or that his lips were pressing kisses along my growing stomach. These are all moments that I'll never get back, at least not with EJ and likely never with Evan. I know Nate is a good father, but missing these things with Evan, knowing how much he wanted the baby growing in my belly at the time he was deployed, pains me that we've missed so much.

Standing here and watching father and son bond, even though they don't realize that's what they're doing, is tearing me apart. Too much pain and agony has been created by someone we were all supposed to trust, and I'm not sure if there's recourse. Even though my son has been brought up by a fantastic dad, he's missed out on a chance to know what an amazing father Evan would've been to him.

I know I can change all that for EJ and for Evan too, but I

don't know how to do it without hurting anyone. The therapist is right: EJ's young, he'll understand. I know I have to tell him, if not for his sake, but for Evan's. He has every right to know his son and be called Dad. He's earned it.

The loud clank of the barbeque lid being shut by my father brings me back to the here and now. Evan is crouched down, talking to EJ whose arms are flying madly in the air. EJ's so animated with everything it's hard for me to tell what kind of story he's sharing. I angle myself just right so I can study Evan's face while he listens to EJ. The smile Evan is sporting is reminiscent to the one he had when I told him I was pregnant. We were so happy I didn't think anything would shatter the bubble we were living in. I was wrong, and hope I can attempt to mend the fixable.

Evan laughs at EJ who in turn bends over and gives him a full belly laugh. My dad and mom chuckle behind me, and I hear my mom sigh. She and I have spent countless nights cuddled together on the couch watching home movies of Evan just so I could hear his voice, so that the baby I was carrying could hear him speak. Even after he died, I didn't stop. Before the news came that he wasn't coming home, I would tell Lois and Frannie all the things we were going to do when he was back. They were annoyed with me, always yammering on, until they weren't because I needed those pretend memories to keep me going. I needed to see in my mind and feel in my heart the way Evan would've held his son, the way he would've coached me during childbirth. I needed to hear him walking up and down the hall at night while he tried to calm EJ down so I could sleep. In my mind he existed.

"Momma, can I show him my room?" The sound of EJ's voice startles me slightly. I'm so lost in a daydream of what could've been that the here and now is standing before me. Evan stands up, reaching his full height and towering over EJ and myself. He doesn't say anything because I feel that he knows I can't deny him. I can't deny him anything, and that scares me.

"His name is Evan," I correct EJ who smacks himself in the forehead.

"I forgot."

"Yes, it's okay to take Evan to your room."

EJ pumps his fist in the air and yells out 'awesome' before he runs off into the house leaving Evan standing there.

"You comin', Eban?" EJ yells, and I find myself laughing at the way he says Evan.

Evan turns and says, "Sure am," before he turns back to me. "Thank you for this, Ryley. I'm not sure I'll be able to express how much it means to me to be here with you, EJ and your mom and dad."

I nod, biting my lower lip. I have to turn away, afraid that his gaze will make me cry. "You should hurry. His room is—"

"I know which one it is, Ry, I remember."

With that, Evan walks into the house that we picked out together. Even though he hasn't been here in six years, he hasn't forgotten a thing. That thought alone makes me think about what he said when he was standing in front of me last week. He had pictures. Someone was making sure that the guys were kept up to date while we were all in mourning. Who would do something so horrible to us and why?

"How ya holding up?" My mom's hands rest on my shoulders.

"I'm okay. Today's been rough, but the therapist helped me realize that it's not Evan's fault and that I have a lot of very hard decisions to make."

"Your father and I are very proud of you, and you know we're here. Why don't you go on upstairs and just watch them interact. It may make telling EJ just a bit easier if he's comfortable around him."

I heed her advice and make my way up to EJ's room. The door is closed, but the laughter coming out of his room is heartwarming. I turn the knob and open the door slowly. My intent is to spy, but what I see just about does me in. EJ is in Evan's arms and he's telling EJ about each picture on the wall. Evan points with his freehand and describes what he was doing and how upset or happy his mom was with him at that particular time. This is really the only moment I've been given, or taken advantage of, to stop and stare at Evan. The memories haven't done him justice, that's for sure. His arms are more muscular, defined really, as he flexes to hold EJ. The tattoos that I had memorized, some that I watched him have done, are there, but less vibrant. His dark hair is buzzed making me miss the locks he had when he left.

Evan points out and names everyone in the photos, and even though EJ knows who they are, he allows Evan to do so. Seeing them together, it's uncanny how much they're alike. The only thing EJ doesn't have is Evan's dark hair.

They turn and find me standing there. Evan doesn't look surprised at all making me wonder if he knew if I was standing here the whole time. He smiles the most adorable lopsided grin, highlighting his dimples.

"Isn't your mom beautiful?" he says to EJ quietly, but loud enough for me to hear. I turn away, staring down at the ground as my cheeks heat up. It's not that I haven't had a compliment in a while, it's just the way Evan says it. His voice has always turned my insides to goo.

"She's pretty," EJ says with a smile. Evan looks at him and grins before turning his gaze onto me. He winks and walks toward me. This is an image I've had on replay in my mind for years. This is how life should be. Not the life we're leading right now, each of us on different sides of the fence with one wanting what he had when he left, and the other learning to move on. We've been dealt a shitty stack of cards.

"Well, I think you guys are both very handsome." EJ nose scrunches up causing us to laugh.

"I don't want to be handsome. I'm cute."

Both Evan and I start to laugh which causes EJ to start as well.

"Is it dinner time?"

I nod. "I think so, but I thought the three of us could talk first."

Evan nods and holds EJ a little tighter. "Where do we talk?"

I motion toward the door. "Downstairs. I know my parents are here, but they know everything and it might be easier for EJ to understand."

"Okay," he agrees and follows me as we make our way back downstairs. I sit first, and Evan sits down across from me. He reluctantly lets EJ go, but I ask EJ to sit down so we can have a talk.

With my hands folded and a frog resting in my throat, I look at Evan and EJ sitting side by side and know it's now or never. Never can't be an option.

"EJ, do you know who Evan is?" I start, unable to really comprehend what I'm saying or how I'm going to tell him.

He looks at Evan, shrugs and shakes his head.

"Do you know how your dad is away right now?"

He nods, still looking confused.

"Evan is your dad's brother, but —"

I have to stop when a sob takes over my body. The couch dips and Evan is next to me with his arms around me. I melt into him. My body knows him regardless of him being away for so long. My hands cover my face as I wipe away the tears. I have to be strong and do this for Evan.

Clearing my throat, I adjust, but Evan doesn't move his arm from my shoulder, and I don't ask him to. It just means I'm going to hell for having these feelings for two men. "You know how Chris has two dads?"

"Yeah, and he says it's the coolest thing 'cause he gets lots of presents." Of course my child would be excited about the prospect of presents and not the drama of having two dads.

"EJ, I know you're only five, but you're very smart and going to start school soon so I want you to listen to me closely."

EJ leans forward with his little arms resting on his knees. Evan chuckles behind me, and all I can think is how much fun it's going to be watching Evan get to know his son and realize how much trouble we're in because EJ is Evan's mini-me in every way that counts.

"Evan is your dad and before I had you in the hospital, he had to go away on a super-secret mission that took a really long time, but he's back now, and he's not going anywhere."

EJ's brows furrow, his expression probably mirrors the one I held when I first saw Evan coming down the steps earlier in the week, although for different reasons.

"EJ?"

He looks up at me with the most confused look I've ever seen. "Are you and Daddy not gettin' married?"

I feel Evan stiffen next to me. I swallow hard and fake a smile at our son. "Your dad and I are still getting married, EJ." With that Evan removes his arm, and I'm instantly cold and left feeling hollow. "What I'm trying to tell you is that Evan is your dad – he helped make you in my tummy – and Nate is also your dad because he's raised you."

I think that I've only confused him more when he blankly stares at me and Evan. Of course, Evan isn't helping, not that I think he should. This is my mess. I need to be the one to clean it up.

My mom and dad walk in, and my mom sits by me while my dad takes the spot next to EJ. He pulls him into his lap and gives him a hug. "I know your mom is making your head all messy, but she's a girl and girls do that a lot."

"Hey," both my mom and I yell out at the same time to no avail because all the men are laughing.

"Do you know your name?" my dad asks, confusing not only EJ but myself as well.

"It's EJ, silly Papa."

"Yes, but what does EJ stand for?"

EJ pretends to think by tapping his finger against his lips, another Evan trait. "Eban junior," he says proudly.

"Well, to have the name junior added, you have to be named after someone and that usually means you're named after your dad and sometimes your mom."

He shrugs, still not understanding. I knew this would be hard, but had no idea that we couldn't convey that Evan is his biological dad, and he's here to stay.

"Sweetie, look at grandma." EJ does immediately and dazzles her with his smile. "Your mommy and Evan were going to get married before he had to go away. Everyone told us that he wasn't coming back – that we'd never see him again – so when you were born, we all wanted you to have a daddy and Nate said he'd do it. Evan and Nate are brothers and Nate – well, we all wanted Nate to help be your daddy."

EJ looks from my mom, to me, to Evan and my dad with his lower lip sticking out. My heart breaks for my son, being five years old and trying to grasp this news. "So he's not my daddy no more?"

"No, of course not," Evan speaks up. "I just want a chance to be your daddy too, EJ. I've missed so much, and I didn't mean to. Look…" Evan moves and reaches for his wallet, pulling out a picture. I catch a glimpse of the photo – it's of me and Evan with his hand on my belly right before he left.

"I know you can't see much, but you're behind my hand, in your mommy's tummy. When she told me that she was pregnant I was so happy… still am happy. I want to marry her someday and had planned to until I had to go away."

It doesn't escape my attention that he said he wants to marry me, not wanted.

"Why'd you go away?"

"My job sent me and… and I don't know EJ, something

happened and I'm not sure how to explain it, but I can promise you that I'll never be gone like that again."

EJ appraises us all to see our reactions. We're all stoic, unreadable. "So I have two dads now?"

All of us nod slowly, except for Evan. I know he doesn't want to agree, but for now this is how it has to be.

"I'm hungry, Papa."

The four of us start laughing in relief. Leave it to the kid to diffuse a heavy situation with a hungry stomach. My dad carries EJ into the other room, followed by my mom, leaving me with Evan who is still sitting so close to me that I could just lean in and get lost in all things Evan. I could pull him close and breathe him in, but that'd be wrong. My traitor body is telling me otherwise though. My skin is screaming to be touched by him and my fingers, they're locked in a vice grip so that I don't reach out and run my fingers over the ink on this arms.

"This is really hard, Ryley."

"I know," I whisper.

"I want my family back, and I'm going to tell you this right now, I'm very angry with Nate. I was told that he knew everything. Hell, I thought you were sending me fucking care packages only to find out you thought I was dead. But there's no excuse for Nate. I've always known he's had feelings for you, and the moment I'm out of the picture he swoops in –"

"It wasn't like that."

"I don't care, Ry. What I care about is you and our son. If I had a choice, I wouldn't have gone on that mission, River and I thought something was up with it when we got the orders, but we follow orders and look where we are now."

Evan stands and places his hand on my cheek, guiding my eyes to his. "I'm going to fight for my family and I'll do it dirty if I have to. I'll be the one standing up at your wedding stopping it, and I'm going to prove that you're still madly in love with me even though we haven't seen or been with each other in six years. Your body sings for me, I felt it when I sat down next to you."

He bends down and places a searing kiss on my lips, and once again I'm back in the ice cream shop with chocolate, raspberry and Evan consuming every sense that I have. I don't want it to end. I want to be sixteen again and starting to fall in love with the most gorgeous boy I've ever met. I want the redo, the start over. I think we've earned that. When he pulls away I almost reach for him, but I refrain. I'm committed to someone else, and the fact that I have to keep reminding myself of that is not a good thing.

EIGHTEEN

Evan

CLOSING MY EYES, I rest my head on the back of the couch. The smell of Ryley's perfume is present and comforting. All night I've been trying not to think about everything I've missed, but sitting at the dinner table with Carole and Jensen acting as if nothing has changed has made me feel split in two. A part of me is grateful that they're not making a big deal out of it, but the other part wants to scream and yell and have them listen to every damn thing I have to say. Thing is, I know Carole will. She'll let me pour my heart out, keep it confidential and try to do something. I'm not sure I want her to have that burden.

Seeing my son in the flesh for the first time is indescribable. I've missed so much, but am thankful to whoever made sure I saw him grow up through photos. When he was standing there holding Ryley's hand, I wanted to break down and cry. I'm not ashamed to admit it. I wanted to sob like a damn baby because my chest hurt. The pain – it's nothing like I've felt before. It didn't matter that he was standing in front of me, smiling. I wanted to fall to my knees and pull him to me. I needed to feel him in my arms and know that he's real and not a figment of my imagination or just an image on a three-by-five piece of glossy paper. Instead, I channeled the warrior in me and held it all together.

Tonight's dinner was by far the best dinner I've ever had. It had nothing to do with the food, but with who was at the table. Sitting next to EJ and watching him barely eat reminded me so much of me when I was a child. Nate was always the hearty eater. Me, I wanted to be outside playing and getting dirty. I'm not sure that's what EJ was thinking today, but food definitely was not on his agenda this evening.

I don't know how Ryley usually handles his picky eating, but tonight she let it go. I'm willing to bet it was because I was here. The last thing I want is for EJ to be in trouble because of my presence, but I also don't want her to waver on her parenting skills. She's going to have to teach me her rules so I can enforce them. I never knew what it meant when people would say it take a village to raise a child, but I do now. It took four of us to explain to EJ that I'm his dad. The child in me wanted to stand up, stomp my feet and tell him that I'm his dad, his only dad and that my brother was crossing the line. But I didn't. I couldn't do that to EJ or Ryley. It's not his fault and as much as I hate to admit it, I'm glad it was Nate over some random man playing daddy in my place. Except, as far as I'm concerned, Nate knew. He should've been protecting my family by being a brother and an uncle, not making plans to take my place.

Ryley sits down next to me, but I keep my eyes closed and pretend that this is normal for us at the end of the night. In an ideal world, I would be cleaning the kitchen while she gives EJ a bath and we'd both tuck him in. We'd sit on the couch and cuddle, or I'd have her feet in my lap while she reads and I'd watch some sporting event on TV until it was time for bed. We'd go upstairs together, and I'd make love to her. Either way, we'd be together, unlike now.

I've never felt so far from her even though she's next to me. When I kissed her earlier I thought I was going to bust out of my seams. Touching her, even with something as simple as cupping her face, brought back six years of anticipation. Maybe it's better this way because if we were to start making out I'd probably blow my load in my shorts and never in my life have I done that.

"How come you haven't called your mom?" her voice is low and calm.

I take a deep breath and think about how best to answer. Why haven't I called my mom? Fear? Anger? I'm not really sure. "I would've, but after learning what I have and hearing Rask tell me about his parents reactions I just haven't been ready, but you're going to change all that for me, aren't you?" I open my eyes and turn my head slightly to look at her. She was watching me the whole time, and I love it.

"We don't get along, your mom and I."

She has my full attention now, so I sit up and pull her hand into mine. I'm looking for any excuse I can find to touch her. "Why not?"

She laughs, but it's not a happy one. Ryley turns to face me, bringing her leg up underneath her other one. She runs her hand through her hair, a tell-tale that she's uncomfortable. "Well, when you died, Nate made sure I received your flag at your funeral for EJ since he knew about us being pregnant. Your mom didn't like that. Nate reenlisted shortly after you passed away. Your mom didn't like that either. The straw that finally broke the camel's back was Nate and I pursuing a relationship."

I squirm when she brings up her and Nate. She has to know I don't want to talk about them, even though I have so many questions.

"I didn't know, Evan. I swear on the life of our son. I would've waited for you." Her voice breaks before she can finish her sentence. I don't really give a shit if she's engaged to another man, I need to hold her. I have her in my arms before she can protest. Not that I think she will. I know she loves me. I can feel it in the way her body molds to mine. We were made for each other and come hell or high water, she'll be mine again. I don't care who I have to hurt along the way to make it happen.

Her tears dampen my shoulder as I hold her in my arms. She cries quietly and my heart races when her hand clutches my shirt. I haven't forgotten her signs. I know what she wants. I could be the man I feel like being and make a move, take her here on the couch, but I won't, at least not tonight. Tonight has been too emotional and when I make love to her again, it's going to be because we can't keep our hands off each other. I'm thinking next week sometime.

I press my lips to her shoulder and pull her tighter to my chest. I need for her to know that I'm here for her and that I'm not going anywhere. I can't imagine I'll be deploying anytime soon considering that someone in the Navy told my family I was dead. They have to know questions are going to start being asked if they haven't already. Carole will no doubt start picking apart our files.

"I'm sorry," she says as she pulls away slowly. I chuckle lightly when she breathes in deeply. She tries to turn away, but I don't allow her to. I guide her face back in my direction and look into her eyes, straight to her soul. Our love is still there, it's just being somewhat blocked by her sense of obligations.

"As much as I want to blame you, I can't. You did what you thought best for our son."

She nods and slips away from me. I feel the immediate disconnect and that just fuels my hate for whoever set this mission in motion.

"How's my mom with EJ?" I ask, changing the subject.

"She's good. Livvie's a good aunt. They just don't talk to me." She shrugs. "I'm used to it."

I don't even want to know what my mother's excuse is for being cold to Ryley, but I'm going to make sure it stops tomorrow. If I hadn't been gone, Ry would be my wife by now and I'd like to think we'd have another child running around the house. I look at her flat stomach and imagine her plump with my child. This time, I'd be here for everything.

"She shouldn't be that way, Ry. I'll talk to her."

Ryley shakes her head. "She has her reasons."

"I don't care. You're the mother of my child and that alone should make her worship the ground you walk on. You gave her another piece of me and as far as I'm concerned that puts you pretty high on a pedestal."

She grins, covering her face. "You always put me on a pedestal."

I lean back so we're almost nose to nose. "I love you, Ryley Clarke, why wouldn't you be there?"

"Even after all these years?"

I adjust so I'm facing her and hold her hand again. "I didn't die, and I didn't know they told you I died. We were getting letters and care packages. Aside from being knee-deep in something horrible, I thought you were waiting. I thought you were sending pictures and letters about EJ and you. We tried to come home, but every time we were told we were done, something would happen and bam we were in the heart of it all again. I wanted to be here. At times I thought about going AWOL, but short of walking into a village and getting captured, there wasn't anything I could do."

"I don't blame you. I blame the Navy. Why did they do this to us?"

I shake my head. "I don't know, babe, but I'm going to find out."

We fall into a comfortable silence, the only sound coming from the clock hanging on the wall. I count each second that she allows me to hold her hand. It gives me hope that she doesn't pull away or choose to sit on the other side of the couch, far away from me. She has to know that I'd want to touch her, kiss her even. What I really want to do is pull her to my chest, lay back and fall asleep with her in my arms.

"I should probably go," I say abruptly, causing her flinch.

Ryley looks from me to the clock and back at me. "Stay."

"Wh-what?" I ask, my voice breaking. The thoughts of being alone with her run rampant through my mind, but I know that's not going to happen tonight. As much as I want to be with her, I don't think she's going to allow me to make a move. Being this close to her though is going to wear me down.

"We have to leave early and it's already late. It seems pointless for you to drive all the way back to base, only to come back here in a few hours."

"Where will I sleep?"

Ryley tries to hide her smile, and by doing so it only solid-ifies what I'm feeling. I have a feeling if I make a move, she'll let me. The thought is tempting, but we're both so damaged I have to make sure my timing is right. Everything has to be natural.

"We have a spare bedroom. I've already made up the bed."

"Show me the way," I agree because I can't be away from her, even if I try.

NINETEEN

Ryley

SLEEP HAS NOT BEEN my friend tonight. The red lights of my clock mock me while the numbers hardly move, yet each time I open my eyes I'm closer to the time when my alarm will blare and I'll have barely slept. I thought having Evan in the house would guarantee me a good night's sleep. I didn't bank on me wanting to sit outside his door or wondering if every sound I heard was him moving around.

The smell of coffee is my final undoing. I know he's awake and as much as I want to deny my feelings, I can't. I don't want to be away from him. Shutting him out earlier this week has been the biggest mistake I've ever made when it's come to him. I should've brought him into our house and made it clear that he belonged here as much as I do. But I let my anger get the better of me. I let the negative emotion control my heart and now I'm paying for it. This past week we could've been finding a happy balance in our lives. Instead, we're walking on egg shells.

A picture of me, Evan and Nate from high school sits on my nightstand, reminding me of the fucked up situation we're in. We were so young when it was taken, we had our lives ahead of us and our futures within our grasp. The twins were so full of themselves, but with good reasoning. They worked so hard for everything, never taking a handout and now two brothers who were best friends are torn apart, and the common denominator is me. I'm hurting both of them. The thought of me being the cause of so much pain shatters my heart and even though Nate's not here so I can talk to him about it, the least I can do is prepare him so he doesn't have to endure the shock and devastation that I have. I pick up my cell phone and scroll through my contacts looking for the emergency number Nate put in there, before hitting the call button and bringing the phone to my ear as I wait for the beep.

"This is Ryley Clarke. It's imperative that Nate Archer call me or come home. His..." my voice breaks, unable to complete the sentence that is going to both destroy Nate and make him so happy. "His brother is home," I say, quickly hanging up. Honestly, they should've notified Nate the moment Evan got back to base. I half expected him home before now. We should probably be doing all of this as a family, but we're not. Nate's not here, Julianne doesn't know and Evan and I are circumventing the issue hanging over us – my impending nuptials. He hasn't asked and I haven't volunteered any information. To be honest, I'm second-guessing everything. I'm not sure how I can marry one man when I'm in love with another. It was one thing when I thought my soul mate was dead, but now that he's a living, breathing human it feels wrong to be engaged to another.

God, my life sounds like a science experiment gone wrong.

I shower and dress quickly, pulling my wet hair up into a bun. This is going to be as good as it gets for me today. Evan gets the make-up-free, messy-haired, dressed-in-yoga-pants-and-a-tank-top Ryley. At least yesterday he had a somewhat presentable version of myself and won't think of me as a total slob. Tiptoeing past EJ's door – I'll wake him right before we leave – I make my way downstairs. My stocking feet mask my entrance into the kitchen, but my sudden intake of breath doesn't. Evan is standing at the kitchen sink with one hand gripping the counter and the other arm bent. I'm assuming he's holding his coffee cup. He's shirtless and his shorts hang low, showing the top of his briefs. His muscles twitch, leading me to believe he knows I'm standing here, staring at him.

Evan hasn't changed much since he's been gone. His muscles may be a little more defined and he may be slightly thinner, but he's still the same. He's nothing like one would expect when reading about a long-lost lover returning and the woman not remembering the man she's shared many nights with because I remember every single thing about him. One of these days I'm going to stop comparing my life to a romance novel or fairytale, but until that day comes I'm going to relish in a little fiction because it helps bury the ache my heart feels.

"Are you going to stand there and stare at me all morning?"

"If you allow me to, yes I am. I've missed you, Evan, and my memories haven't done you justice. I can't hide those feelings or turn them off." I'm not sure where the sudden confidence comes from, but I like it. I know that keeping everything bottled up isn't going to help us or me. I need to open up, regardless of how much it's going to hurt me, him and Nate. The fact is, we've been thrown into a complicated situation with no answers. Our lives are being turned upside down with hearts shattering.

His back holds my gaze as he lifts his cup to his mouth. Every muscle in his back moves creating these obscene ripples, making my heart race. He laughs, knowing that I'm standing here and staring. He remembers my fascination with his body and is using it to his advantage.

I huff and walk over to the coffee pot only to find my cup already poured. Closing my eyes I try not to let this small gesture or the smell of his cologne get to me. He's done this many times before and he wouldn't know not to do it because he hasn't been here. It's still habit for him. I know he's being the Evan that I love, but I'm committed to Nate. I can't let my love for Evan taint what Nate and I have built. I just can't, even though I have no doubt everything with Evan would be so much better than it was before.

"Who'll watch Deefur while we're gone?"

He says "we're" and I try not to show him that his words have any effect on me. After taking a sip, I set down my mug. "Lois and Carter will. They don't live far." He stiffens, and I'm sure it's at the mention of Carter who is Nate's best friend. Everything from now on will be nothing but awkwardness.

"They're still together?"

I nod. "Yeah, they have a daughter, Grace. She's a year younger than EJ."

Evan chuckles and pours the rest of his coffee down the drain, running water to watch away the residue. "I'm sure Lois already has EJ marrying her daughter."

"You know it," I say, following his actions. "Did you go back to base?"

He turns, resting his hip against the sink. He smiles as his eyes rove over me. His hand comes up, pushing a piece of hair behind my ear. The chills are instant and as much as I want to fight my response to him, I can't.

"I needed to shower," he says slowly and I'm reminded that he said he planned to play dirty. I look away, swallowing hard, only for his finger to slide under my chin to bring my face back to his. He leans forward, and I know he's going to kiss me. I should move away, but I'm telling myself that he has a hold of my face, so I can't.

Evan's hand moves gently across my face, his fingers spreading wide as he holds the back of my neck in the palm of his hand. His lips are soft and move easily across mine.

Everything about this kiss is familiar, yet so very new and unexpected. As much as I want to keep going, I can't. When I pull away, his lips rest against my forehead as my hands clutch the waistband of his shorts.

"I'm not sorry," he whispers against my skin. "As far as I'm concerned, we're together. We didn't break up unless you want to break up with me now." He pulls back and looks at me with a glint in his eye.

My head shakes slowly as he kisses me again. "I love you, Ryley," he says before leaving me standing in my kitchen, with my heart speeding after him. It would be so easy to fall back into a routine with him, and I wish that I could without consequences.

"Can we go dere?" I look out the window to see what EJ is talking about. We've stopped in traffic and set up not far off the road is a carnival, or maybe it's a country fair.

"Not today, but we will when we get back."

"Promtise?"

"Of course, I do," I tell him as I look back at him riding in his seat. Evan insisted on driving in case EJ needed me. I think he secretly wanted to watch EJ in the rearview mirror because each time he fell asleep, Evan was slipping his hand into mine. I'm not fighting the affection. I know Evan needs it. I also know it's wrong. I should keep my space because I'm engaged to another man whether he wants to accept it or not.

"Remember when we went to the fair?"

Yes! I want to scream at the top of my lungs. "Our second

date," I say, shyly, remembering exactly what our date entailed. That night, I saw just how romantic Evan could be.

"Do you remember the Ferris wheel?"

I try not to smile, but can't help it. "I remember." I stare at the Ferris wheel and feel slightly jealous of the kids up there, doing what Evan and I did. "You thought you were so smooth."

Evan laughs, but keeps eye contact with me. "I was smooth. You had me on my toes. I had never met anyone like you. Every thought I had from the moment we met was about you."

I hold his gaze, relishing in his admission. I'll never be able to fully describe how he made me feel.

"I remember that day perfectly, Ry. I was holding your hand and said, 'Do you want to go on some rides?'"

I shake my head, recalling that day all too well. "Those rides made me cringe. I looked at the large hunks of metal and thought how can those rides be safe? They take them down and put them back together so many times. 'No, thanks.' I said, but was screaming on the inside to get me out of there, take me to the cows, anything, except those rides. You put your arm around me and pulled me closer. I felt so safe walking through those crowds and when you stopped in front of the photo booth I had a mild panic attack."

"Why?" he's trying not to laugh, but I can see the glint in his eyes. He's mischievous bringing up this day. I squint at him, letting him know that I see through him. His innocent act isn't fooling me.

"Once you closed those ugly maroon curtains I blurted out 'What are we doing?' I wanted to bang my head against the wall for being so stupid. I completely sucked at the dating thing. Of course I knew what we were doing."

"You didn't suck, Ry."

"No, that part came later, right?" I raise my eyebrows at him, earning a crude gesture in return.

"'Well, for starters I'm going to sit you on my lap.' That's what I said to you, I believe. Your expression was full of questions until I pulled you right on top of me. I had to touch you so I slid my hand under your shirt. I remember your skin pebbling and I thought 'damn, this girl is going to be the death of me.' But when you leaned in, I knew you were feeling the same as I was."

"'Now, I'm going to kiss you.' That's what you said. I was so eager I couldn't wait, so I kissed you and I remember feeling you on my leg. Knowing that you were turned on didn't scare me though."

"'And now we're going to take pictures.' God, I was so cheesy. Why didn't you go running for the hills?"

"Because I was already in love." My admission catches him off guard. He picks up my hand, even though he knows EJ is watching and kisses my wrist.

"I knew you were the one," he says, breaking my heart just a little bit more. "I still have the photo that was taken of me looking at you. I carry it everywhere."

"Everywhere?" I ask.

He nods. "Even in my helmet. When it was taken, I thought, 'Wow, how did a dumb jock like me get so lucky?'"

My smile fades as tears prickle my eyes. I won't cry, not now. I turn and face the carnival again and let his words replay again.

"'I want to take you on the Ferris wheel. The view from the top, overlooking the city, is amazing and you need to see it.' That's what you said. My dad told me earlier that night to watch out for pick-up lines, but I didn't care."

"'Do you trust me?' That's what I asked you, and you said yes so damn fast. The first time we went around and you saw the city, you gasped. I couldn't believe how excited you were, but your dad was right; that was a pick up line because I wanted to kiss you senseless, and I thought it'd be romantic at the top of the Ferris wheel."

"You said I was beautiful."

"You still are, Ry."

"I couldn't take my eyes off you once you said that."

"Nor could I keep my lips off of you. That night, you let go and gave me the sexiest kiss I've ever had."

I laugh, remembering all too clearly what it felt like when our tongues met for the first time. Forget fireworks, I was a full on grenade of teenage hormones. "I was eager after that," I say, looking back at him.

"Shall we pull off and relive that date?" he laughs as I turn red.

"EJ..." I say shaking my head. Everything is different. We're not kids anymore. I look over my shoulder and watch him stare at the fair. He loves the kiddie rides and can easily wear me out with a day at the fair.

"Someday, Ryley," he says as we start driving again. Someday seems like it could be tomorrow or years from now. Either way, *someday* is going to be filled with heartache and pain, tears and hurtful words. I continue to stare out the window at the passing scenery and count down the miles until it's my turn to drive.

TWENTY

Evan
___

TEN HOURS IN THE car with the love of my life and I can't touch her, say the things I want to say or pull over on a deserted road to show her how much I love her. Ten hours in the car with my son, who doesn't know me, placates me by answering my questions when asked and doesn't make eye contact with me because to him, I'm just a man driving his mom's car who he's been told is his dad. Needless to say, the Archer men are wound up, confused and ready to be out of the metal confinement we're in.

Being in the car, traveling with Ryley and EJ, regardless of the destination has been surreal. The talking, the laughter and the subtle touches when she'd brush my arm with hers to hand something to EJ are all moments that I'm storing in my memory bank. Each moment is one I'll cherish because I don't know if or when I'll get more. We may get to my mother's, drive home and she could tell me that I'm no longer welcome or that I can see EJ once a week. Thing is, I want to see her every day. I'm not sure she understands how deep and solid my love for her is. EJ is a product of our love. He makes us complete. I can't have him without her. Life doesn't work that way for me.

Recounting our day at the fair gives me hope. Knowing now that she was in love with me then tells me that winning her back may not be so hard. Thing is, Ryley's loyal and I'm not about to do anything to compromise her integrity. I should probably stop kissing her, but I can't. I don't want to. I need her to know that I'm in this for the long haul or until she decides that my brother is definitely the one for her. I know he's not though. He's too straight-laced and soft to keep someone like Ryley happy. You wouldn't know it by looking at her, but she craves the danger, the excitement. She likes the bad-boy façade with the nice guy on the inside. That's who I am and have never been anything different. I'm the rule breaker, the rebel, but at night you'll find me cuddled up next to her. Or I soon will be.

I see a lot of me in EJ already. I've noticed the looks he gives Ryley when she tells him he can't do something. The defiance is there just waiting to come out. When I was little, probably around his age, my mother called me the devil and always referred to Nate as her angel. It didn't bother me until now. Looking back, even my dad favored Nate. Maybe it's because I was more outgoing or wasn't afraid to go after what I wanted. I don't know. Either way, the more I think about it, the angrier I become.

Exiting off the highway, my heart begins to beat just a bit faster and my palms start to sweat, but not in the way I get when see Ryley. This is from nerves. In hindsight, I should've waited until after Rask saw his parents, so I'd be able to gauge their reaction and prepare myself for what my mom and sister are going to do. I could've called her, but after Rask's mom ended up in the hospital with a minor heart attack, I didn't think that'd be a good idea. Frankly, dealing with all this bullshit with Ryley has been enough to keep my mind occupied. I'm a shit son for not calling, but my life is upside down right now. Hopefully my mom will understand.

I look over at Ryley as she watches the passing scenery.

Her arm is sitting down by her side and I keep telling myself it's because she wants me to hold her hand. Fuck it. I need to hold her hand. I need her comfort and support. Grasping her hand in mine, she looks quickly at me then over her shoulder at EJ, who from the rearview mirror I can see isn't paying attention to what his mom is doing. He should see his dad touching his mom. It'll give him a healthy perspective when he starts dating. It just sucks that he doesn't know me as his dad. Hopefully he will in due time, but I can't rush him. It'd be incredibly selfish and unfair of me to make him call me 'Dad' or even consider me as such.

Driving through the streets of Sacramento, I'm surprised that I remember the way to my mother's. She moved here after Livvie graduated from high school. Nate and I tried to convince her to move to San Diego so she'd be closer, but she said it'd be too hot and was tired of being so close to the water. I don't blame her, with my dad dying and all, but with EJ being around I sort of hoped she'd be near him.

Her relationship with Ryley is one that concerns me. I've always had visions that my mother would be there every step of the way for my kids and my wife. Ryley may not be my wife... yet, but she's the mother of my son. EJ is the innocent one here. I'm not saying she has to live near me, but the story Ryley tells doesn't fit the mold I had for my mom as a grandma.

"You should pull over so we can talk before we get to your mom's."

I do as she suggests, not really questioning her. I'm sure she's nervous, and for different reasons. I put the car in park, and turn slightly to face her.

"Last night I told you that your mom and I don't get along, and as much as I would rather stay home today, I feel that you need some support. We were all very angry, very bitter. I think that after she lost your dad, she became jaded and when you... well, when we were told that you were gone she just shut down. She's not the same person you remember."

I process her words and for one moment try to put myself in their shoes but I can't. If I were told that Ryley were dead, I'd drink myself into oblivion until I could join her. I don't want to think about her ever being gone from my life, even though, technically, it feels a little like that now. Physically I can see her and touch her. I can hear her voice and smell her coconut shampoo. My mom can't do any of that with my dad, and she couldn't do it with me after she was told I was gone.

"I also think I should go in first and tell her so that she's prepared. I don't want her to be like me and say horrible things to you when she sees you because she doesn't believe."

"Okay," I agree with her instantly because I think she has a point. I don't want to relive that afternoon with Ryley. The memory of that day is a hard pill to swallow. I pray that I'll never witness that much fear, resentment, and unknown by her again

I put the car into drive and head down into the cul-de-sac where my mom lives. The white house with blue shutters is decorated with hanging flower baskets and rose bushes. I pull into the driveway without thinking, only for my mother to step outside in her gardening clothes.

"This isn't going to be good. She's going to think you're Nate," Ryley says, hopping out of the car.

"Hi, Julianne." Her voice is muffled and as much as I don't want to, I crack the window open a little so I can hear clearly.

"This is a surprise." My mother's voice is clipped. I don't like it. She knows how far Ryley's traveled with EJ to get here, she should be happy. I grip the steering wheel to keep myself from jumping out of the car to yell at her. That wouldn't do any of us any good.

"I have some news, Julianne, and I need you to sit down."

My mom leans to the side to look into the car. "Is Nate going to get out or are you two running off to Vegas?"

"No, please sit down."

Mom throws her hands up in the air, as if she's brushing off Ryley. I see her move toward the car and know that I need to get out before she gets to the driver side door.

"Julianne, please," Ryley pleads to no avail.

I make the conscious decision to get out of the car and pray she doesn't collapse onto the ground.

"Nate, get out of the car and come see me. I may not agree with your wedding, but I'm still your ..."

Her eyes meet mine and her mouth drops open. Ryley moves in behind her, maybe to catch her or keep her from running. She turns and looks at Ryley who now has tears streaming down her face. Ryley nods, confirming my mom's silent question. With her gaze back on mine, she shakes her head and her own tears begin to fall. I stand stock still, afraid to move.

"It can't be," mom whispers as she covers her mouth.

Ryley sets her hand on my mom's shoulder. "He's real, Julianne. Everything you thought... you were right."

I make a mental note to ask Ryley more about what she just said, but for now I take a deep breath and address my mom. "Hi, Mom."

"Oh, God."

She buckles, but Ryley is there to catch her before she hits the ground. I slam the car door and am by her side instantly. I scoop her up in my arms and head toward her house. Everything I'm doing now I wish I did with Ryley, but her reaction was nothing but anger, and I completely understand that now.

Ryley and EJ follow us in. He's at his grandma's side the moment I set her down. She cups his face and he gives her multiple kisses on her cheek before he runs off down the hall.

"Such a sweet boy," she says without making eye contact

with me or Ryley. "I told you that you and Nate were a mistake."

Ryley shakes her head and takes a seat across from us. I grab a hold of my mom's hand and tug a little so she's look at me.

"Mom, I've missed so much and have a lot to make up for, so I'm asking that you not bring up Nate and Ryley right now."

"She told you?"

"Of course she did," I defend Ryley.

Mom wipes angrily at her tears. "How long have you been alive?"

I run my hand over my hair and smile. "About thirty-five years."

She laughs and so does Ryley. "I see you haven't lost your sense of humor."

I relax a bit into the couch and put my arm on the back of it. "About a week and before you start asking a bunch of questions let me tell you that no, I didn't know we were all dead. I think we were part of a cover-up gone badly, and whoever was leading it is somehow not involved anymore because we were brought home. The entire time I was gone, I received care packages. I knew just about everything about Ryley and EJ, except for the obvious. I was also under the impression that Nate knew where I was. I was told many times that my brother knew about the mission, so needless to say I was a little taken aback when I came home to find out I'm dead and my fiancée is no longer mine, but my brother's."

Mom nods and lets the tears free fall. I pull her into my arms and tell her that I love her. "Everything's been so hard since you left."

"I know," I whisper. "But I'm back and I'm not going anywhere. I have a girl to win back and a son to get to know." My words make her stiffen and she pulls away from me.

"You intend to take Ryley from your brother?"

"Yeah, I do."

"And you're going to allow that to happen?" she directs her question to Ryley, who sits stone faced and unanswering.

"Mom, Ryley didn't leave me, nor did I leave her. She was mine and when I came home, I flat out expected a fucking homecoming, but instead I find out that my brother moved in on my family instead of protecting them like he vowed to do."

"Nate would never do anything to hurt you, Evan."

"Yet he did."

"You were dead. What was he supposed to do?"

I throw my hands up in exasperation. "Geez, mom, I don't know, not covet my fucking girl."

"Watch your mouth."

I shake my head. "I think I've earned the right to drop the f-bomb after the shit I've been through." I can't sit any longer. I stand up and start pacing, stopping and looking at the mantle of dead servicemen. I want to take mine down and throw it against the wall, but that's something I'll save for my mom.

"Are you really my son?" her voice cracks as I nod.

"He is," Ryley says. "And before you go assuming anything, you should know that Evan and I started therapy this week, and we're trying to find a peaceful resolution."

I shrug. "Ryley's may be peaceful. I intend to fight."

"They're getting married, Evan; surely you don't want to ruin their wedding."

I glance from Ryley, who knows exactly that's what I plan to do, to my mother who is going to bat for Nate and realize that everything Ryley has said is true. "Mom, when I left she was my fiancée. We didn't break up, so as far as I'm concerned she's still mine."

"Oh, Evan, everything is so much more complicated than that."

"I know about EJ and Nate. EJ also knows that I'm his dad. I'm not expecting things to change overnight, but I am expecting some changes. I didn't die, mom. My life didn't stop. I didn't lose my memory, and I wasn't held captive. I came home and thought my family was waiting for me. I was wrong, but my family is trying, and that's all I need right now. You can be on Nate's side all you want, but as far as I'm concerned he's dead to me. All he had to do was protect Ryley and EJ. Instead, he thought he'd take advantage of the situation."

"He thought you were dead," she roars, protecting him. "We all did." She points to the mantle behind me. "It's not like he made a conscious decision to go after Ryley. Believe me, Evan, I begged him not to. I begged her not to. But as I've been reminded many times, they're adults and they fell in love. Don't blame your brother when he's not here to defend himself."

She stands and glares at Ryley before leaving the room. This homecoming isn't going like I thought it would. Hell, none of them are. Maybe I was better off being dead.

The tug on my shorts cuts short my pity party. I look down to find EJ staring at me. "Hi, EJ," I say, unsure of what I should call him. I'd like to call him buddy or junior, but don't want to if that's what Nate calls him.

"Can you come outside and play wif me?"

I glance at Ryley, who's nodding. "You bet," I say to EJ, who takes my hand and pulls me through the house to the backyard that holds a nice-sized jungle gym.

TWENTY-ONE

Ryley

I DON'T KNOW IF I expected Julianne's icy demeanor toward me to change when she saw Evan, but I definitely didn't expect her to sling a verbal attack my way to take the blame off of Nate. When Nate and I were growing closer, no one more than me tried to put the brakes on our relationship. It just grew, everything just happened. You reach a point where there's no turning back because if you do, you lose your best friend and I couldn't afford to lose him too.

I still can't afford to lose him. I know I will eventually. There's only so much one person can take, and the moment he finds out that Evan is alive it's going to be a fight or flight situation. He either stays and fights for EJ and me and could lose us all, or he leaves and it's EJ and I losing. We're in a no-win situation and have the Navy to thank for it.

Someone is to blame for Evan being gone for so long. Someone needs to explain why we were told he and everyone else was dead. Someone needs to pay and take the blame for this mistake or whatever it is they're calling it. We need answers and guidance. We need reassurance that this will never happen again. I need to know why they sent care packages on my behalf but watched as I mourned the love of my life. Who does that to people?

"Mom kick you out?"

Livvie comes into view. She looks more like Evan than Nate and it used to be hard to look at her. When she was younger, we got along well. She was the sister I always wanted, but never had. I used to have her antagonize the girls Nate would bring home. I never thought any of them were good enough for him except for Cara. She left when he wouldn't leave the SEALs after Evan died. I know she was scared – I was too – but it's no reason to turn your back on the one you love.

I look away from Livvie and roll my eyes. I don't want a confrontation with her, but I know one is coming. She hates me. I don't blame her. Not only did I give Nate the green light to go back to active duty, I did the incomprehensible to her by being with him. She told me that I was desecrating Evan's memory. She's probably right, and it makes me wonder if that is how Evan feels now.

"Is EJ here?"

"Yeah, he's here… with Evan."

Livvie pauses mid-step. She sets her foot down and slides into a sitting position. "What'd you say?"

I sigh and lean back so we can make eye contact. "I know you're angry with me and I don't blame you, but I need you to hear me out before you walk inside that house. The other day I came home and Evan was there."

She gasps and covers her mouth.

"He was walking toward me like he had done so many times before when he'd come back from deployment. Except as soon as she saw my face, he knew something was wrong. As far as he knew, we thought he was alive. He was getting care packages that were marked from me, from you and your mom. He had no idea we had buried him years ago."

"You're telling me that my brother, who we buried, is alive and in my house?" she points the house and I nod.

"With his son."

"What?" her voice breaks. "You told EJ that Evan is his dad?"

"What was I supposed to do, Livvie? Tell Evan that since he died he doesn't get to know his son? He died, we moved on. We all agreed that we'd let EJ call Nate dad because we didn't want him to feel left out in school. Well, now look at us. Evan isn't dead, Nate's not home and EJ has no idea what the hell is going on!" I throw my hands up exasperated. It's been a constant battle with her and Julianne. If it's not one thing, it's another. It doesn't matter what I do, they're never satisfied with the results.

The screen door opens and I know it's Evan before Livvie realizes he's standing there. "Hey, Tink," he says from behind us. I look over my shoulder and smile. He's standing there with his ball cap on backwards and his hands pushed into his pockets. This is the Evan that left us all those years ago. We've lost so much time and because of that lives have been damaged.

"Evan, is it really you?" Livvie asks as she stands on shaky legs. She climbs the few steps to where he's standing and he pulls her into his arms. She's crying into his shoulder and this makes me realize that this is the first emotion he's received from any of us. The rest of us are too shocked by his return to let this side of us show. That is how my reunion should've been with him. Instead I threw myself a pity party and didn't invite him.

"It's me, Tink," he says as he lets her go. "I'm sorry I missed your graduation," she snorts and pushes into him.

"I'm sure you can make it up to me. My God, Evan, you... I can't even say it. What happened?"

Evan takes Livvie's hand and leads her back down the stairs. He sits next to me and motions for her to sit in front of him. Her eyes widen when he takes my hand in his. I glance at him to read his expression and from what I can gather, he doesn't care what she thinks.

"Livvie, I'm in love Ryley and always have been, you know that. I didn't die out there. I wasn't captured or lost. I was working and the whole time I was out there, I thought my girl was waiting for me. So when I come home and she's freaking yelling at me, I figure she hates me. Except that's not the problem. Not only does she think I'm a ghost but she's engaged to my brother. I didn't give her away, Tink. I'm going to fight for her."

"What about Nate? I'm not trying to pick sides here Ev, but Nate's been there for her and EJ the whole time. EJ thinks Nate's his dad and he's a damn good dad. You can't just take that away from him."

"I won't. I can't do that to EJ. But I'm not going to stand by and lose my girl to him when I don't deserve that."

"That's true, you don't," she mutters. Livvie takes a moment to look at her brother before she leans into him, resting her head on his knee. "I can't believe you're alive. Do you know many nights I cried for you? How many Mom did?"

He shakes his head while running his fingers through her hair. "I can't imagine what you guys went through. Had I known, I would've tried to get word to you."

I scoff at this statement because from what we've learned there was no way they were letting the fire team reach their families. Someone wanted these guys gone.

"What, you don't think he would?" she asks incredulously.

"It's not that, Tink. Believe me when I tell you this, Ryley isn't upset that I'm alive, just confused, as we all are. Four of us were sent out on what was to be a routine pick up and they didn't let us come back. Each time it was something else. The mission continued to grow until one day there's a chopper to bring us back. We had no idea what was going on when we got back to base. No one filled us in. There wasn't an immediate debrief. We didn't have any family waiting for us. We are just as much in the dark as you right now."

"It just doesn't seem fair," Livvie says, wiping away a tear. "We've lost so much."

Evan and I both nod as he brings my hand up to his mouth, kissing it gently. Livvie gasps just as my heart starts racing again and I hold my breath waiting to see what he does next.

This isn't what our homecoming should be like. I shouldn't be afraid each time he touches me. I should be holding on to him, clinging for dear life and not be afraid to admit that I miss him the second he moves away from me or walks out of the room. Each time he does leave my sight, I stop holding my breath and gasp for all the air I can get before he returns.

"Nate's going to freak," Livvie blurts out. Evan shrugs and I turn away, trying to pull my hand away. I'm in the most fucked-up situation ever and belong on one of those shows where they sit you in the middle and each guy rips you apart with a verbal attack on how you destroyed their lives. That's what I deserve.

"I called and left a message for Nate to come home, or at least call me." The words spew out before I have a chance to realize that Evan probably doesn't care, evident by him stiffening next me. I notice his less-than-subtle attempt to release my hand, but I play his game and don't allow it.

"What are you going to say to him?" Livvie asks the question I know is on Evan's mind.

I shrug and look away from both of them. "It's not going to matter what I say, everything will sound the same."

"He's going to be pissed," she adds, trailing off.

"Who gives a fuck?" Evan mutters. He's shaking slightly, allowing the anger to take over.

"Evan," I blanch. "He didn't choose this for you, you have to know that."

He shakes his head, clearly not believing me. What I don't get is why they'd tell him Nate knew and why he thinks Nate wouldn't tell us, or try to bring him home. There are so many lies surrounding this mess that I fear we'll never have our answers.

"I can't help it, Ry. I just can't. I'm so angry I could kill him right now." I turn and glare at him, ripping my hand away from his grasp. He moves too quickly for me and has me by the waist and pulled against his now standing form. "You don't understand, Ry." His forehead rests against mine and I feel the need to succumb to him right then and there.

"Well, explain it then."

He shakes his head. "If he were in my platoon, he'd be dead for taking you away. I'm trying to wrap my head around why he did this knowing where I was."

I cup his face, feeling his stubble against the pads of my fingers. "Evan, he would never be dishonest to either of us that way. If he knew, he wouldn't have allowed us to bury you. He would've gone to my mom and told her. I don't think he knew."

Evan leans back and looks me square in the eye. I search his for any semblance of understanding or acceptance but there is none. I've seen Evan and Nate argue before, even not talk to each other, but what I fear happening between them now is going to destroy this family again beyond repair.

TWENTY-TWO

Evan

———

PACKING UP AT FOUR A.M. again is not my cup of tea, but watching Ryley uncomfortable and awkward and listening to my mother make snide comments about her isn't either. I'd much rather lounge around and get to know my son, but I can do that anywhere. As long as Ryley lets me back in the house to do so.

I want our time together to be a stepping-stone in reconnecting. It doesn't ever escape my mind that she's committed to another, and while that should stop me, it doesn't. I should be a gentleman, but it's not in me. I'm a fighter and she's my top prize, my damn salvation. Without her I'm nothing.

Ryley comes out of the spare bedroom with her fuck-me cut-off shorts on and her hair piled on top of her head. I reach for her, cupping her ass with my hands and am about to kiss the shit out of her when my mother's door opens. I don't move away after being caught with my hand in the cookie jar and meet my mom's glare with my own.

"She's Nate's," she mumbles, walking by.

"She's not a piece of property," I reply, staring at Ryley. I lean forward and whisper in her ear, "Except you're mine."

She punches me lightly in the chest. "I thought I wasn't a

piece of property?" Her eyebrow raises and all I want to do is kiss the fuck out of that smirk of hers.

"Eh, I lied." I swat her ass lightly and walk into the guest room. EJ is sleeping in the middle of the bed with his arms spread out wide. "Does he always sleep like this?

Ryley brushes against me and intentional or not, I'm taking it. "Yes, reminds me of someone else I know." She smiles before turning away.

"It's not my fault that I have to touch you while I'm sleeping." I scoop EJ up and into my arms. He's a dead weight, but feels light as feather. I have so much to make up for and hope that he gives me a chance. Maybe we can toss a football around later, or a baseball. I'll do anything he wants as long as I get to spend some time with him. Unless he's into dress up – not sure I can handle him putting make-up on me. We'd have to tag team Ryley and decorate her.

I think back to what I just said to Ryley about touching her when I sleep. It's been so long that I'm not sure I remember what she feels like pressed up against me. My memories probably have nothing on reality. It's been so long since I've had her in my arms like that.

"You ready?" her voice breaks my reverie. I smile at her and double check EJ's car seat not remembering if I strapped him in or not.

"Yeah," I nod. My mom comes outside to say goodbye. She doesn't hug Ryley and that really irritates me. Ryley could've been a bitch and kept EJ from her, but she didn't. The least my mom can do is respect her and treat her fairly. I give her a quick one arm hug and slide into the car. I refuse to make eye contact with her as I start the car and pull out of her driveway. I do, however, link hands with Ryley and wink at her. She shakes her head, but allows a sly little smile to form on her cute mouth. I'm really starting to despise our life right now. There's so much I want to do to her, but that fucking ring on her left hand is stopping me. I have far too much respect for her to even put her in that position. I have no respect for the man who slipped it on her finger though and I'm going to do everything I can to get it off and out of her life.

After a quick pit stop for coffee and breakfast, we're back on the road. We could've eaten at my mother's, but I wanted to get out of there and wish we flew instead of driving, although sitting next to Ryley for an extended period of time is well worth it.

"I'm sorry about my mom." I don't know why I feel the need to say this, but I do. I want her to know that it doesn't matter what my mom thinks or says. I still love her. Probably more now than I did before I left. I'm not sure how that's possible, but it's how I'm feeling.

"It's fine, Evan. It's something I've been dealing with since… it's just been awhile."

She avoids saying that I died and I'm thankful for that. It's beyond creepy to hear her say that to me. I know she's having a hard time, but so am I.

As we drive, I keep looking over at her. She's reading with her feet on the dash. Her toes are painted electric blue and her feet are moving to the beat from the radio. If she were anyone else, including my sister, I'd slap her legs down. I hate seeing feet on the dash. My eyes travel between her legs and the road. I have to adjust the way I'm sitting and in the process her hand brushes against the bulge forming in my shorts. Her eyes catch mine and I slam my hand down on hers before she can pull away. My eyes close briefly and the images of our first time together flash before my eyes.

I knew she was a virgin when I met her. It only took me a day to figure it out, but it never bothered me. That wasn't why I was with her. From the moment I met her on the street, sprawled out and bruised from my errant throw I was smitten with her. There was something about her that I couldn't get off my mind. I had to have her.

She was so cautious with me though because other chicks in school bragged. I wasn't a saint, not like Nate. He was saving himself and I was sampling the variety in front of me until Ryley came along. I know she thought I was a player, but I only had eyes for her from that moment. It took me a long time to convince her that I didn't want anyone else. I never thought she'd be the one to initiate sex though and when she did, I just about blew my load right in my gym shorts.

One of Ryley's rules, or rather her father's rule, was that she wasn't allowed at my house unless my parents were home. Most of the time, it wasn't a big deal because my mom was always home. She'd let us go up to my room as long as the door stayed open. That really didn't mean anything because she never came upstairs. She had no reason to. Nate and I were responsible for keeping the upstairs clean and once I started bringing Ryley over, I busted my ass up there.

My parents were out of town and I told her, mostly to tease her. I didn't expect her to want to come over. When she asked if we were going to my house I remember looking at her with so much surprise I couldn't come up with the answer. When she pulled her lower lip in between her teeth and looked up at me. I lost it. I knew she was ready or willing to try. That all our heavy make-out sessions were finally going to help me round that last base and head for home.

When we pulled into my driveway, my head was swimming. It was like my brain was gasping for air, and I couldn't clear the fog. I couldn't understand. Here was my girl, ready and willing to give herself to me in a way she can give to no other, and I couldn't think straight. When my dick should have been doing all the thinking, he was laying limp in my shorts. "*Fucking asshole.*"

I held her hand in mine as we climbed the steps to my room. Once she crossed the threshold, I shut my door quietly, even though no one was home, and turned the lock. I didn't want Nate walking in or thinking I was in here alone. Her back was facing me and I used this to my advantage.

I moved her hair to the side and kissed her neck, her collarbone and then down to her shoulder, sliding the strap of her dress and bra down the side of her arm. I repeated the same steps on the other side, all the while listening to her breathing heavily. I knew the moment that she hesitated I'd stop. If she wasn't ready, we'd wait.

She turned and jumped into my arms, her lips smashing against mine. I was fumbling to remove her dress and she was taking control, showing me how eager and ready she was. We flopped onto my bed, both of us groaning for all the wrong reasons and still fighting to get our clothes off.

I felt out of breath when I finally sat up and yanked my shorts down, springing free. I was so happy when my dick was alert and ready. He had me worried. That was until Ryley sat forward and took me in her hand. My eyes rolled as her hand worked to get me harder.

There I was sitting on my knees, watching my girl stroke my cock all while she's naked in front of me, waiting. She knew what she wanted and pulled me forward, guiding me to her entrance. I wanted to take her so bad, right then and there, but I paused and she knew something was wrong. I didn't have any condoms and I was mentally kicking my ass for being this fucking stupid.

'I love you, Ryley, but we can't do this.'

'Why not?'

'I don't have any condoms.'

'I'm on the pill, Evan. I want this with you.'

Who was I to deny my girl what she wanted?

"Where'd you go?" she asks, bringing me out of my own porn film.

I shake my head. "Just remembering our first time together." She blushes and looks away, but doesn't move her hand from my lap. If I didn't know better, and I can't confirm this without looking down at my crotch, I swear to god her pinky is rubbing up and down over the outside of my pants making me wish our son wasn't in the back sleeping.

"We were so young."

I shake my head. "You were. Technically, I was an adult."

"That was so long ago."

I pick up her hand and kiss her before placing in back on my thigh. She looks at me when her hand brushes against me and I wink. She has to know that she still has this effect on me. I don't want her thinking that she doesn't turn me on just by sitting next to me.

"We were stupid," I throw out there, thinking about how we never used a condom.

She looks over her shoulder and I wish I could see her eyes right now. I want to see them light up when she looks at our son. "I don't know about that, Evan. We created him."

"Babe, we created him ten years after being together. I'm talking about when we were teens and screwing all over the place without a condom."

This time she shrugs. "If I had gotten pregnant back then, what would you have done?"

"Same thing I did when you got pregnant with EJ. Ask you to marry me." I have to look away because by all accounts we should be married by now. I should've made her an honest woman years ago, but our lives were too busy.

"It's what I should do now."

"It's not that easy," she whispers and yet keeps her hand on my leg.

"Ry, the quicker you realize you're not marrying Nate, not as long as I'm alive, the quicker we can move on with our lives."

Her head turns sharply, and I know I'm in trouble. "And what makes you think I'm not going to marry Nate."

"Simple, you love me."

TWENTY-THREE

Ryley

NATE STILL ISN'T HOME and each day that passes brings me closer and closer to the brink of panic. I've called and left another message, more urgent than before. I don't know if he's getting them or not, but it concerns me that whoever's delivering them isn't doing so with the intent of an emergency. I want Nate to hear it from me that Evan is alive even though I wouldn't be surprised if someone in his company has already informed him.

And if that's the case, why isn't he home? Why isn't he here dealing with everything that I am? I know that once he's here, things will go from relatively calm to utter chaos. My life is slowly becoming a bad segment on a talk show. Two brothers, as close as any brothers could be, will battle it out over me and my son. Lines are already drawn in the sand so to speak, and EJ and I are standing smack dab in the middle. It's not going to matter which side I step to; the Archer twins will never be the same. I could choose neither, but I know deep down that Evan will never accept that. And neither will Nate. They both love me, each in their own way. I feel like I'm on a cracked out version of *The Bachelorette*.

Evan has been staying here since the day we finished our

first therapy session. That was over a week ago. I didn't have it in me to send him back to the base, especially since this is his house and he's trying to get to know EJ. I'm not gonna lie, having him here has been hard. I've had to sit on my hands one too many times to keep myself from touching him. Every hand hold, every kiss, every moment we've shared has been initiated by him. I have no doubt he's questioning my love for him, but I can't bring myself to disgrace Nate that way. I know I should tell Evan to knock it off, but I can't. I love him. I have since I was seventeen and having him here, in the flesh, is a constant reminder of what I've been missing.

The moment I saw him walking toward me when he first got back, the hole in my heart started to fill up again. That was the pain I was feeling that day, along with the fear that I was only imagining him standing before me. I was afraid this was all a cruel joke and that he was going to disappear the very second I touched him. It's why I couldn't accept that he was real, that he was back from the dead. No one would ever be that callous. But they were. Someone sat by and watched my, and others', world crumble without a second thought. Now they're sitting back and watching us try and rebuild the lives that have been destroyed.

Evan places his hand on my shoulder and the automatic reflex of my head resting on top of his happens. I close my eyes and feel the warmth radiating off of him. As soon as he pulls away, my eyes are open, and I'm watching our son drive around the backyard in the toy Jeep Evan bought for him. I told Evan he can't buy his love, and he assured me he's not. He's just trying to make up for missed birthdays.

When Evan walks in front of me, I gasp and quickly cover my mouth. He sits next me and pulls my hand away from my mouth to hold it.

"What's wrong, babe?"

He knows what's wrong, but is going to make me say it

anyway. "It's the NWU's. I didn't think... I don't know what I thought."

"I'm still enlisted, Ryley."

I nod, knowing this, but I didn't think I'd see him wearing NWU's any time soon. "I know, Evan. I'm just a little taken by the sight, that's all." I try to recover, but the wavering is there. If I had my way, he'd retire, but I know he has to be on active duty if he wants to find out what happened to him and the guys.

"I told you, I don't think they'll send me anywhere. Our unit is too much of a risk right now. Did I tell you that Frannie is going to the paper?" I shake my head. "She says this mission was a cover up for something big and people need to pay. She plans to take it all the way to Capitol Hill to get answers."

"Do you think she will?" I look at Evan and he looks hopeful. Answers won't change our situation, but they might give us some closure.

"I'm trying to remain optimistic."

I smile at him before turning my attention back to EJ. We have our first joint counseling session today and we're just waiting for my dad to get here. I was hesitant to even go to therapy, but have to admit, she made me think about a lot of things in my life. One thing that's giving me a lot of pause is my upcoming nuptials to Nate. Honestly, I'm not sure getting married to him, or anyone at this point, is the right thing to do. I need to find myself and get over my anger of having lost six years with Evan.

"Hey, you still with me?" he shakes my hand, bringing me out of my funk.

"Yes," I say, stretching my legs out in front of me to get my blood flowing.

"Your dad's here, we should go." Evan stands, pulling me up by my hand that he won't let go of. I'm thankful EJ doesn't ask me why we're always holding hands because honestly I won't be able to give him an answer. I kiss my dad on the cheek as we pass and continue to allow Evan to guide me to the car. It's my car, yet he's driving. I guess some things never change.

Evan and I climb the stairs to the therapist's office, hand in hand. I'm starting to think he's glued to me. I'm not complaining, but think this might be awkward for the doctor. Not that Evan will care. As soon as we're in the waiting room, the receptionist directs us into the same room where I fell apart, emotionally and physically.

We step in and I'm instantly hit with the sun shining through the window, bouncing off the pale yellow walls and making the artwork shine. I look around confused and wonder if we're in the same room as before.

"What's going on in your head? Evan asks.

I shrug. "This room looks different," I say as I take a seat in one of the two chairs in front of her desk. As I look around, I notice fresh flowers by the window and picture frames containing the doctor's various degrees. On her desk, the nameplate reads Helen Howard. It's odd how I didn't notice this before.

"I was thinking the same thing. This room was gloomy and this chair hurt my back. Hell, I didn't even know she had a name." he mumbles right as Dr. Howard walks in. She smiles as soon as she sees our joined hands, and I know she's getting the wrong impression.

"It's good to see you both again. I take it things are going well?"

Evan nods, while I shake my head. And there it is, our first disagreement. Her face falls and her eyes look again at our hands.

"We're not together, if that's what you're implying," I inform her.

"Not yet, it's only a matter time." I roll my eyes at his confidence.

Dr. Howard folds her hands and rests them on her desk. "Shall we get started?"

We both nod and I cross my legs, directing my foot toward Evan so I can kick when I need to.

"Who wants to start?"

"I do," Evan answers her before I have a chance to. He adjusts slightly in his seat. "I don't know what you said to Ryley in her session, but I want to thank you. If I could kiss you without harassment charges being filed, I would do so. That night," he takes a deep breath. "I met my son and had dinner with Ryley, EJ and her parents. It was literally the best night of my life, and I'm hoping to have with more nights with them. But, Ryley is upset with what I'm wearing, and I don't know how to help her be comfortable with my job without damaging what we're trying to rebuild."

Dr. Howard looks from Evan to me after she makes her obligated notes.

"Ryley, do you want to talk about that fear with Evan?"

"Sure." I'm not sure what I can say to alleviate the fear that is bubbling in my stomach. What if we're back together and he has to leave again? I'm not sure I could handle it. I couldn't when I was seventeen, and barely could when he left six years ago. Over time, I learned to accept and move forward, but now… I'm not so sure I'd be able to.

"I'm scared," I say. "When he walked outside dressed like this, I was suddenly in high school again and he was leaving." I shake my head and reach for a tissue.

"She tried to break-up with me," Evan adds lightly. There's nothing light about him leaving, ever.

"How did you feel, Ryley, when Evan told you he enlisted in the Navy?"

I take a deep breath and squeeze his hand. "Lost, confused. Proud. I honestly didn't know what to expect. I knew this was Nate's plan long before I came into the picture, but Evan and I never really discussed his future. I was losing my best friends at the same time and my only saving grace was that I'd have Lois."

"Did you and Evan break-up before he went to basic?"

I half choke and laugh, remembering how he wouldn't allow me to. "No," I shake my head and look over at Evan. He has a smile plastered all over his face because he knows how well this moment in our lives ended. "I thought we'd break up, ya know? I mean he was going off to work and didn't need some needy teenager pining away for him. I didn't want to be that girlfriend, so I broke up with him. I remember the night perfectly. It was one week before he was set to leave. We went to the park and I just blurted it out. '*I think we should break-up.*'"

"I asked her if she was nuts," Evan adds for good measure. He leans over and kisses me on the cheek. "I love you, babe," he whispers sending chills down my arms.

I take a calming breath and continue. "I didn't want him to feel obligated."

"Did you, Evan?" Dr. Howard asks with her pen poised for more notes.

"Never. I didn't see Ryley as an obligation or anything like that. I saw her as my future and still do. I told her that I loved her more than anything and wanted the whole world to know. I told her that at basic I was going to need to know that my girl was going to be on the other end of the line when I got a chance to call. I needed to know that when she read my letters she felt the same way. I wanted her there when I grad-uated, but only if she wanted to be."

"I did," I say, chocking on a sob. "I wanted all that too, and we had it."

"The day he left, Ryley, how did you feel?"

God, what's with the hard, emotional questions already? Can't we ease into things? Again, I'm sitting here and don't want to answer anything. Even with Evan sitting next to me, I'd rather just talk to him and not give her an intrusive insight into our lives.

"I was a wreck. I still wasn't sure that staying together was the right thing for him, and when it was time for me to meet him at his house so I could go with him, I stayed at home. I sat on my bed and cried. He burst through my door and scooped me up in his arms. He was crying, and I knew I had made a mistake."

Evan clears his throat and I glance at him. My heart aches for the pain I'm causing again. He holds unshed tears in his eyes all because of me. "I asked if she was having second thoughts and that if she was, to not tell me until I came home. I wouldn't be able to handle basic knowing that I lost her."

"What'd you end up doing, Ryley?"

"I went. I cried. I held on until it was time for him to go and waved like a lunatic when the bus pulled away." I clear my throat. "That night, Lois came over and we watched movies and ate ice cream. She said we were treating my aching heart like a bad test grade. Lois reminded me that Evan was returning home, and when he did he'd be a full-fledged sailor with a uniform." I laugh now, but back then all I could think about was Evan's uniform and how the thought of him in one made my heart race.

Still does.

TWENTY-FOUR

Evan

———————

LISTENING TO RYLEY TALK about how she felt when I was leaving for basic training really does a number on me. I'm that tough guy you read about – the one who doesn't cry or show emotion no matter what's happening. You learn to be like this, it's taught to you. It's what makes you stand out above the weak. But for the life of me, I can't keep the tears at bay when Ryley relives the time I was leaving. We hadn't been together a year, and I fully expected us to stay together. By all accounts, our relationship was backwards. It was me who thought about a future when it should've been Ryley. She never begged me to stay, only encouraged me to go.

Breaking up wasn't an option for me. I had a life planned out for us, and I saw Ryley playing the part as my partner, best friend and my better half. Being at basic training with a girlfriend wasn't unheard of, but a lot of the guys in my barracks didn't have one so they didn't understand that I wasn't whole, that a part of me was still back at home wishing I was there helping her get ready for her senior year. Knowing Ryley was waiting for me is what pushed me to excel. I wanted to make her proud.

I pull Ryley into my arms and hold her. It's really just

another excuse to touch her, but knowing that I'm comforting her helps me try to make everything okay. I don't regret enlisting. I regret not questioning my last mission, but there isn't anything I can about that now.

Ryley pulls herself together and removes herself from my arms. The loss is felt immediately, but is easily rectified when I grasp her hand. Dr. Howard smiles, but quickly turns her head away. I'm certain that she doesn't want to show any sign of approval on what I'm doing, but I'm certain that's what her smile means.

"Evan, what was it like being away from Ryley?"

I clear my throat and look Ryley in the eye so she can understand what I'm about to tell her. We've never discussed my time at basic. It wasn't something we needed to talk about when I came home.

"Being away at basic training was easy. I had a goal and was going to achieve it. During the day, thoughts of Ryley were the last thing on my mind. I focused on the task at hand. The classes. The push-ups. The runs. I pushed myself hard to succeed. My recruit division commander knew my dad, so he was hard on me. I welcomed it. When I was alone though, or had some downtime, she was all I thought about. Every thought was a memory from the past year and visions of future memories we were going to create. I'd listen to stories of other guys and see if I could picture Ryley and myself in their situation. Some I could and others, there was no way."

"Like what, Evan?"

"Like her being pregnant and me being away from her. One of the guys had gotten his girl pregnant. He joined the Navy so that he could provide for his family. That's an admirable thing to do, but it wouldn't have been for me. I wouldn't have been able to stay away."

"But you left when she was pregnant with EJ," Dr. Howard points out.

"I may have a double standard here, but if I'm eighteen

and my girl is pregnant because I didn't wear a condom, I'm going to stick around and help her. When Ryley became pregnant with EJ, we were trying for a baby and I was already invested in work. My job is just like yours." I look at Dr. Howard when I speak. "You go to work and heal people. I go to work and save people. Different job, same result. My office is all over the world. You can't cancel your appointments whenever you want and neither can I.

"Finding out she was pregnant changed my life. It kicked my ass. I asked her to marry me, which honestly should've happened years prior to that. As soon as I was done with basic, I should have proposed and we should've gotten married. I was taking her for granted. And that's something I promise never to do again."

"You're very noble, Evan." If I didn't know any better, I'd call Dr. Howard a romantic.

"I'm not, Doc. I'm a man in love, and I have been in love with her since I was eighteen. Being gone for six years hasn't changed how I feel about her, regardless of her wearing another man's ring."

Ryley shifts when I mention her ring. I'm counting down the days when she'll be removing it and putting mine back in its place. It's where it belongs.

"How do you feel about Ryley and Nate?"

I stiffen and so does Ryley.

"I really don't want to talk about Nate," Ryley mumbles. I agree with her. He's not a topic that I really want to discuss. Dr. Howard rests her hands on her desk and looks at us.

"Hard truths will help you pave the path for the future, whether you guys end up together or not. If Ryley or you, Evan, don't communicate and get all your feelings out now, this could come back to bite you. You've both told me how you feel, but you need to tell each other. I'm gathering that neither of you have openly discussed that part of her life."

I shake my head slowly while biting the inside of my

cheek. I'm not sure there is anything she can tell me that will take away this stabbing pain. Each time I hear about her and Nate, I feel like I'm being gutted and a pack of wolves are feasting on me. I hate thinking that she's slept with anyone but me. I'm not a possessive man, but right now I feel like I am. I want to go all caveman and pound my chest while speaking broken English and pointing out that she's mine. She always has been and if I have anything to say or do about it, she will continue to be.

"It's not like I meant for –"

I pull my hand from her and raise it. "Stop," I say. Truth is I don't want to hear any excuses. It's happened. Neither of them can take it back. Her, I'm willing to forgive. Him, I'm not even willing to try. "Anything you say can't change the way I'm feeling. I feel like a broken record, defending myself over and over again. I didn't die. I can't control what the Navy does to me. I went off to do a job and when I came home, you moved on. To me, it's like you've cheated. I know you were told I was dead, I get that, but it doesn't and won't change the way I feel about you or this situation."

I can't bear to look at Ryley when I hear her choke on a sob. My heart is racing, beating so fast with the energy I'm feeling that it's making me agitated. My leg starts to bounce and I have an urgency to release this pent up aggression, but I can't do it here. Not in front of Ryley. The thoughts I'm having about Nate will scare her. The devastation I want him to feel, the anger and hurt that I want him to live with, don't even come close to what I'm feeling right now.

"Evan?"

My eyes turn sharply to Dr. Howard. She sits there calmly, knowing that I won't do anything to upset Ryley. If Nate were here that'd be a different story. I can guarantee you that I will not attend any session if he's in the room.

"Look, I get that we have to talk about him, but maybe today isn't the best day. These past few days with Ryley and

EJ have been a blessing, and I'm not interested in having a shitty attitude the rest of the day because we had to discuss the one thing keeping us from being together."

"You're already angry," Ryley mumbles.

I turn toward her. "Of course I'm angry, Ry. I want to be with you. It's damn near the only thing I think about when we're on watch. Being next to you, hell being in the same vicinity as you, only increases my desire. I'm trying to respect that ring on your finger, and it's killing me, especially when I want to throw you over my shoulder and carry you up to our room. So yeah, I'm angry."

I turn away from her and bend at my waist, holding my head in my hands. With my eyes closed, I'm breathing in and out, calming myself down. Her hand touches the small of my back and heat radiates through my shirt and onto my skin. Does she feel the same way? Or have I suddenly become expendable?

"I'd like to talk about the time Evan came home from basic training." Ryley's voice is soft, but determined. I remember the day perfectly. I rest on my elbows, but can't bring myself to look at her. I want to hear this story, so I'm going to sit here and listen.

"Go ahead, Ryley."

"It was homecoming, and I wasn't going to the dance. Lois had tried to get me to go with her and Carter. He was coming home for the weekend, but I didn't want to be a third wheel. She kept pestering me and made sure I was included in all her shopping festivities. I remember telling Evan that I thought she was being a little annoying and that I was very okay with staying home. He told me to go and have fun."

"And did you?"

This time I glance at Ryley and smile. She nods. "I did, but under protest. The night of the dance I decided that I didn't want to go and that it was going to be too much since I had gone with Evan the previous year." She shrugs and looks at me, her eyes twinkling with the memory of what awaited her. "I didn't want to go to a school dance without him.

"It didn't matter though because Lois all but dressed me, did my hair and dragged me to the dance. When we got there, the music was playing, and I started to scope out a spot along the wall to sit. As I started walking in that direction, the lights went out and two spotlights came on. One was focused on me and the other a little ways away. Lois whispered that I need to follow the light, so I did."

"I was waiting for her," I pipe up. "I had come home the night before and wanted to surprise her. Our moms and Lois helped me plan everything. I wouldn't have been able to do it without them."

Ryley smiles as I reach for her hand and lean back in the chair. "We talked for an hour or more each night," she says.

"It's unheard of, spending that much time on the phone while at basic, isn't it? Did you think that was odd?"

She shrugs. "I was relishing in the moment, I guess. I found out later that he had graduated a week earlier, but wanted to surprise me."

"What happened next?" Doc asks.

"The spotlight guided Ryley to me and once she reached where I was standing she jumped into my arms."

"He was so handsome, decked out in his dress blues. I didn't let go of him that night and broke my curfew. Rules be damned when Evan came home to see me."

Doc Howard hands Ryley a tissue, and I watch as both of them dab their eyes.

"That was very romantic, Evan."

I shrug. "Ryley made it easy for me to be romantic. I had never done a grand gesture like that with anyone before, but with her it's something I thought about doing all the time."

I lean over and place my lips just below her ear. Ryley leans into me, allowing me to hold her against me. When she does things like this, it makes me wonder just how committed she is to Nate or if he was simply someone to fill the void that I left behind. I could ask her, but putting her on the spot won't earn me any valuable points and right now I need a stockpile of them if I'm going to win her back.

"I love you, babe," I whisper before righting myself in my chair. Our hands, once again, linked for good measure.

TWENTY-FIVE

Ryley

_____

I WANT TO SAY today's session was a breakthrough, but I'd be lying. When we arrived I was hopeful. Walking into a room that I dreaded last time felt different, almost refreshing. It was as if I wore sunglasses last time. I had a sense of calm and understanding this time.

Today, I wanted to be there with Evan. I thought we'd be able to make some headway, but wounds were torn open, both his, mine and ours. It's a process; I think we both know that. I was foolish to think that one additional session was going to fix us. I had hope. I thought that I'd feel somewhat better. I don't. I know I'm hurting Evan each day that I wear this ring. I'll be hurting him more if I make the decision to keep wearing it. I'm hurting Nate, even though he's not here, by thinking about a life with Evan, dreaming about the life we should've had.

Maybe I should go away. That might be best for everyone involved. EJ and I could find happiness elsewhere in some other state. He's young enough to adapt... my thought about EJ adapting stops my thought process. If I'm so willing to leave and have him adjust, why can't I force the issue with Evan being his father?

Because I'm a chicken shit, that's why.

Evan drives, winding us through the streets leading back to our house. The sun is bright and bearing down on my face as I lean partially out the window. The air conditioner is blowing, but I want the wind in my face. I'm sure it's irritating Evan, but right now I don't care. I feel like a kid again and it feels amazing.

"Do you remember that one time–"

"That you went to band camp?"

I roll my eyes and sit up straight. "You just had to go there?"

Evan laughs and turns down the radio. "I couldn't help myself. Babe, we must've watched *American Pie* over and over again until we had it memorized."

"It was dumb. When Jim humped the pie I really thought you and Nate were going to try it." I laugh at the memory, but my mood quickly turns somber when I mention Nate. I shake my head, clearing my thoughts. "Anyway, it's a good thing I never let you try to whole flute thing."

Loud laughter quickly fills the car, and I can't help but join in. "You know I was joking, right?"

"I know, although at first I thought you might be serious. We had just started dating when you said it. I got a little scared."

"You know I'd never do anything to hurt you or make you uncomfortable, right?" Evan reaches across the console and rests his hand on my leg. This is the first time he's touched me since we left the therapist's office. His fingers graze the inside of my thigh, creating a wave of goose bumps. I love the sensation, and honestly wish I could do something about it. I make a mental note to call and leave Nate another message. He needs to come home so we can deal with this together.

"You still with me?"

I look over and smile at Evan. He's not watching me, he's watching the road, which I suppose is a good thing since he's driving. I use this moment to study him. Since he's been home I haven't really gotten a very good look at him until now. He's lost weight, not a considerable amount, but noticeable. His jaw line is more defined and prevalent. His hair seems to have a hint of gray. I won't be able to tell for sure until he grows it out. His arms, one of my favorite features, are bigger but not bugling. You can tell he's lifted a lot of heavy objects but not weights.

Sitting here watching him, the urge to trace his jaw strikes me. I fold my hands in my lap to prevent me from reaching over to him and keep up with my staring. I'm sure he doesn't mind because surely he knows when eyes are watching him. That's what he's trained to know. I want to run my fingers over his hair and feel the prickly sensation I used to get after a few days of growth has appeared after his buzz cut. I can see him now, closing his eyes as I rub his head, him melting into my palm as my fingers move softly over his scalp. I used to be able to lay there for hours and just run my fingertips back and forth, letting the softness lull me to sleep. He never once complained.

"You're thinking about touching me aren't you?"

If I didn't know better I'd say he's a mind reader, but that's not the case. He's a freaking pervert and only has one thing on his mind. I shake my head and turn my gaze out the front window. We're close to the beach, in the opposite direction of our house.

"Where are we going?"

"You didn't answer my question," he retorts.

"It wasn't a question, Evan; it was a statement that I'm not going to dignify with a response."

"Ah, she wants me," he says as he starts tickling my leg. I have to grab his hand with both of mine to get him away.

"Stop, Evan, you're going to crash the car."

"Just admit it."

"I won't."

Evan pulls into the parking lot and slams the car into park. He relaxes his hand allowing me to release my grip. "Admit it."

I shake my head.

He slips his hand behind my neck and pulls me closer. "Admit it, Ry," he says huskily making my palpations rise. I swallow hard and refuse to let him win.

Evan pulls me forward, crashing his lips to mine. Before, our kisses have been simple and sweet. This is the opposite. The moment his tongue touches mine, I'm transformed back in time. I'm sitting across from him in the ice cream shop. I'm next to him the Ferris wheel. We're lying on a bed of blankets looking at the stars. He's in my room, slowly undressing himself and me before he lies next to me. We're in the grass, with this hand on my stomach and he's asking me to marry him.

My hands grip the back of his neck, my nails digging into his skin. He moans, and my body begs to be touched by him. I'm lifted out of my seat. My back is pressed against the steering wheel and I'm no longer a women in my thirties, but seventeen and horny. Willing and ready to get into the backseat just so I can feel my boyfriend inside of me.

"We have to stop," I say against his lips, but make no effort to push myself away from him. He senses this and pulls me in deeper. Hands are everywhere. His. Mine. Skin is touched and burning with desire. His thumb brushes against the valley of my breasts and I lean in, aching for his touch, missing the way we were.

"God, Ryley, I fucking want you."

My nails rake through his hair. I grind against him, feeling his bulge press between my legs. We've been here before, down this path. The end result is what I want, but I can't have. He knows this. I know this.

I pull away slowly already missing the way my lips feel when he's kissing them. His eyes are hooded and his breathing is labored. He's at his tipping point. I carefully try to extract myself from his lap, but his hands clamp down on my hips.

"Don't move," he says as he rocks his hips into mine. My eyes roll back as I bite down on my lip and meet him with each thrust. "Tell me you don't want me. Say the words, babe, and I'll stop."

I brace my hands against his shoulders, my lips against his neck. I trail kisses up until I reach his ear and gently pull his lobe in between my teeth. "I do want you, but I can't. Please don't pressure me to do something I'll regret."

TWENTY-SIX

Evan

_____

MY BREATH QUICKENS WHEN she grazes my neck, her teeth pulling on my ear lobe. This is her telltale sign. I know her body more than she does. I unleashed the sex kitten that she is. I trained her, honed her. My hands grip her hips as I press into her. I don't care that it's broad daylight and we're in a parking lot. She could easily slip off her shorts and straddle me. I want this woman. She's the only one I've ever wanted.

But she stops me. She doesn't tell me no. Ryley tells me that she wants me, but can't have me. She asks me not to make her do something she'll regret. It's that word that makes me stop, but I don't allow her to move. I want her to feel me. I need her to remember what it's like for us, when we're connected the way two lovers should be. I want her to know what she does to me with just her presence. This woman owns me: mind, body and soul.

I want her to cheat on Nate. I'm not ashamed to admit something like that. I want him to know that she's mine. She always has been and always will be. The only time he's stood a chance is when he thought I was dead. Simple fact is, I've been gone for six years and I miss my girl. I need to reconnect with her on every level and hate that I have to because of a decision that was made. I don't want to respect her choice. I want to be that asshole that doesn't give a shit about anyone's feelings but my own, and right now those feelings are dictating my thinking ability.

"Ryley, if you don't want me to take you right here, right now, please stop tugging on my ear." I hate that I have to beg her stop. Any other time, and she'd be naked and writhing underneath me. I've never seen anything or anyone as sexy as Ryley when she's sated.

She stills and tries to move away. I only asked her to stop, not leave my lap. I happen to like the feel of her pressed against me. It's the worst kind of torture and pleasure wrapped into one.

"I'm sorry," she whispers against my neck before she rests her head there. I don't have a clue as to why she'd be sorry.

I wrap my arms around her and hold her to my chest. She sobs quietly while repeating how sorry she is. Maybe this is a breakthrough for her, or maybe I needed to remind her what we're like together. It's not that we just connect, we become one. From the first time we were together, we've been able to anticipate each other's needs, wants and desires. Never has she had to question if she was doing something right or if I liked something. My body and my actions told her everything she needed to know.

"Please don't be sorry."

"But I am. I feel like I'm leading you on and that's not my intent. I've missed you so much and I want to be with you, but I can't."

"You can, but not yet," I remind her. We may not be able to be together right now, but our time will come. I have no doubt in my mind that she'll tell Nate that she can't be with him and choose me. I'm not willing to think of a different outcome. She's all I know, all I want.

"You're so confident."

I flex, showing her how confident I am. She leans back, her eyes red-rimmed, and it breaks my heart. I bring my fingertips to her face, wiping away her tears. "I love you, Ryley. There isn't anything I wouldn't do for you, to win you back, to show you that you're meant to be mine. And as much as I love having you sit on my lap, the guys are on the beach and we're going to eat by the fire and hang out. I already set it up with your dad to watch EJ so we can just hang out with our friends."

"I haven't done one of these since the night before you left."

"Not even with –"

She cuts me with a shake of her head, and I'm thankful. I never thought I'd cringe at saying his name, but I do. Aside from being brothers, we were best friends, unit mates. I could always count on him to be there when I needed him, and he felt the same way about me. At least that's what I thought. But to hear that he never took her to the beach for a party or an outing sends waves of relief through me. This is still something she and I did, and he hasn't tainted it.

"Well, I guess he's earned a point."

"Evan," she drags my name out, her voice full of disappointment. I can't help it. Whenever I think of them together I see red, and maybe a hint of green. No, I take that back. I see a lot of green. I'm jealous as hell that he's spent the last six years with my girl while I've been fighting a losing battle in the jungle. And for what? There hasn't been a resolution or even a debriefing on what we did over there. It hasn't even made the news, nor have we been called in and relieved of our duties. A small voice tells me I should probably fear for my life right now. What if whoever is in charge considers me or the other guys a threat and takes us out?

I try not to linger on that thought. The last thing I want to do is alert Ryley that anything may be amiss, but it's definitely on my mind.

"I don't know what you want me to say, Ry."

"He's your brother."

"He was. I don't consider him as such anymore. If he were acting as my brother, he wouldn't have placed his ring on your finger. He would've stood by you, helped you raise our son as his nephew, and been there when you needed him. Pursuing you is crossing the line. I'm also having a hard time understanding how it is he knew about my location, but had no qualms trying to make you his."

"What if he didn't know, Evan? Have you thought about that? You're holding all this anger in, and he may have not known." She pleads his case, something he should be doing, but hasn't had the balls to come home and do. Your brother coming back from the "dead" should be enough for any commander to relieve you of your duties and let you return home. Yet, he's not here. Maybe it's because I called him last night and told him if he knew what was best, he'd stay gone. That could backfire though because I need him here so Ryley can dump his ass and restart a life with me.

"Obviously we don't have the answers, babe. But what he did? That alone is enough for me to disown him."

Ryley leans away from me, her back pressing against the steering wheel and her arms crossed over her chest. I glance around quickly, looking at the people passing by, keeping my eyes anywhere but at the scowl on her face. She pulls my chin in her direction and I can tell she's pissed, which is fine because I've been in a perpetual state of pissed offness since I returned. I think I'm entitled to feel this way.

"What if I sought Nate out? Have you ever stopped to consider that it might have been me who went after him?"

I study her for a moment before my head starts to move back and forth. "Are you telling me that you've had the hots for my brother? That while we were together you secretly longed to be with him? Told our mother that you could do better than me?"

"What... no," she blanches. *This* is exactly how I know he went after her and not vice versa.

"My point exactly, Ryley." I push her hair behind her ear and caress her cheek. "I don't want to fight about this. Right now, I want to go hang out with my buddies, our friends. I want to have a good time and just relax and pretend that everything is normal."

"Okay." She hesitates a beat before answering with a smile while removing herself from my lap. I groan as I watch her ass wiggle in her stupid little shorts before climbing out of the car after her. We walk hand in hand to the beach, both of us carrying the necessities that I had hidden away in her car.

River and Frannie are already set up and it's comforting knowing that she and Frannie are so close. River and I hug it out before both popping open a cold one. He pats me on the shoulder and motions for me to follow him down the beach.

"How are things going?"

I shrug. "They're all right I guess, considering the situation. Nate hasn't come back yet, and I'm not sure if he's staying away because he knows I'm going to beat his ass or what."

"Man our lives are so fucked right now." River tips back his beer and takes a long pull. We stand, facing the ocean with our feet buried in the sand. This is the perfect place to talk because the waves drown out our voices. If anyone is lurking, we'll be hard to hear.

"I talked to Ryley's mom today," River starts and immediately has my attention. "She's been digging and it's not pretty, but she's afraid to cause waves at the moment. She wants more evidence."

"What has she found?"

River looks around and over his shoulder. "Our files were pulled months before we left, each one flagged. The initial mission was never logged. There's no evidence that we went to Cuba. Everything about us being there..." he shakes his head. "Nothing. There's nothing until they notified the families that we were dead. Our files were then transferred and that's it."

I look at him dumbfounded. How are all the logs not there? The extractions? "What about the kids we put back on those Hercules'?"

River shakes his head. "There's no record. Clarke even searched for the kidnapped child and found nothing. There never was a police, FBI or CIA report. You'd think if a child of a U.S. Senator is kidnapped the damn media would be all over it, but there's nothing. And all those children we rescued, no records."

"Where the hell did they go?"

He shrugs and empties his beer. "I don't know, Archer, but I don't like it. Whatever we were told to do, we contributed to a crime."

I stand there in disbelief, questioning my commitment to the Navy. Maybe it's not the Navy I should be questioning, but our CO. Where the hell is he? I turn and look over my shoulder at Ryley; she's sitting in a chair talking to Frannie.

"How's that going?" River tips his head toward Ry.

"It's... difficult. I have fucking blue balls as in I really think they're starting to turn fucking blue. I feel like I'm looking at a damn skin mag every time she walks in a room and we just had a serious make-out session in the car. It's fucking high school all over again."

River laughs, earning a stink-eye look from me. "Is she shutting you down?"

I nod and tip back my bottle. "It's that damn ring. If it wasn't there I wouldn't hesitate, but I know if she goes that far she'll have regrets and that'll be bad for me. I've already pushed my luck with her, and she's cheated on him. At least in my eyes she has."

"Do you think Nate's not coming home because he's

waiting for her to screw up? That would give him an easy out."

I tip my bottle back and empty its contents. "He's going to come home acting like he had no idea I was alive and be hurt. Shit thing is, my mom is on his side and kept reminding me that Ryley's his. I beg to differ. That woman up there with your wife was made for me. It's just a matter of time before I have her again."

"Frannie likes her. She was there for her and EJ. She said it helped her cope with my death."

"Man, this shit is so fucked up," I say as I slam my empty beer bottle into the sand. "We've missed so much and for what? Nothing, that's what, and no one is going to pay for the shit we've missed."

River pats me on the shoulder. "Rask and McCoy are here. Let's head back up there and start the bonfire."

We walk back up the beach and as soon as Ryley sees me, her eyes light up. I don't care what people think of me right now, this girl is mine. I either need to be patient or take that damn ring off her finger myself.

I sit down next to her and place my arm around her. She leans into me, warming me instantly. I kiss the top of her head, letting my lips linger there for longer than necessary but not long enough to satisfy me.

TWENTY-SEVEN

Ryley

WATCHING THE SUNSET OVER the Pacific Ocean can only be summed up with one word: breathtaking. It could be the company I'm in, or simply the view. Either way, the pure beauty that is enveloping my friends and me tonight gives me peace and a lot to think about. The more time I spend with Evan, the more I know I'm meant to be with him. He's been home for almost two weeks, and it seems like it was just yesterday. We have so much to re-learn about each other, and he about EJ, but each day is like Christmas and we're unwrapping presents one at a time.

The fire crackles in front of me as the guys and Frannie sit around and tell stories from years that have gone by. We don't talk about the past six years. Most of us are trying to pretend they don't exist. We all want answers but none of us have them. Evan told me earlier that my mom has been looking into why this happened, but is afraid of snooping too deep without proper evidence. I don't blame her. I have a feeling this is bigger than any of us combined and if someone can make four men from a SEAL commando disappear, they can do anything to the rest of us.

"What if they come after us?" I blurt out before I realize

168

what I'm saying. All eyes are on me instantly, and even though it's dark I can see almost everyone's eyes piercing through me. I swallow hard and look at Evan who's staring at the fire with a scowl on his face.

"Don't think like that, Ry," Evan says firmly, and I know I've hit a nerve. McCoy opens a new beer and downs it without stopping. Frannie is looking at me, and River is staring at the fire. Rask is rubbing his head, and Evan's leg is bouncing.

"I can't help it and by the looks on everyone's faces, you've all thought it too. Someone made you guys disappear for six years. You just don't come back from the dead without there being repercussions." I angrily wipe away a tear that's falling down my cheek. I'm trying to be strong here, not weak and emotional. I've never feared for my life, but this situation is giving me a lot of concern. If my mom is investigating, someone is going to find out. That someone could want to remain anonymous and the easiest way to keep a secret is to eliminate the person or people who know. They'd have a lot of blood on their hands, but their secret would be kept.

"I think about it," Frannie says. "I see lights shining through our bedroom window at night and wonder if someone is going to knock on the door." River reaches for her hand to comfort her. "During the day, I'm constantly looking over my shoulder and brushing off people who ask questions about your return. I don't trust them."

"Neither do my parents," Rask adds.

"How'd your meeting go?" Evan asks him, reminding me that Rask met with his parents while Evan and I were at his mom's. I should've waited to take Evan home so we could stay and support Rask. That was a very selfish move on my part.

Rask shrugs and kicks some sand around. "My mom..." he shakes his head before covering his face. "She doesn't believe. Says I'm an imposter, a clone. She's convinced that

I'm not her son and that hers was buried a long time ago. It didn't matter what I said to her, or how many memories I recounted, she wouldn't budge. I tried to hug her, but she recoiled and hid behind my dad.

"He didn't say anything either. I finally gave up and left. I couldn't sit there and watch them shun me over something I had no control over."

I cover my mouth and hold back a sob for Rask. "I'm so sorry, Justin." Frannie reaches over and grabs his hand, but he lets go quickly.

"Today's Claire's birthday. She's nine and I'm not there to celebrate with her," McCoy says somberly.

"Do you have any leads?" River asks, but McCoy shakes his head.

"I have nothing. Claire isn't enrolled in school anywhere under her name. Penni isn't working and if she is, it's under a different social security number. I'm starting to think they're dead, and I just don't want to believe that they don't exist. Why would Penni need to hide? None of it makes sense."

The mood quickly turns somber after McCoy's declaration. He stares at the fire, his eyes glazed over. I can't help but feel sorry for starting this conversation, but it's been weighing on my mind.

"Penni never came around after the funeral. I went over a couple of times, just like I did to check on Ryley, but no one answered. About a week after, people were there cleaning out the house and there was no sign of her or Claire. I asked, but was told they didn't know anything. I wish I remember the name on the side of the truck."

McCoy's head pops up. "Do you think you can remember if you saw pictures?"

"Yes."

"No."

Frannie and River answer at the same time. She looks at him questioningly, but his eyes are focused on McCoy.

"Ryley has brought up what we've all been thinking. We were dropped on an airfield and our CO is conveniently missing. Her mom has been snooping around, but isn't ready to break into anything, and your wife and daughter are missing, McCoy. I think it's all related, and I don't want Frannie involved until she has to be. She and Ryley, they need to stay as far away from this as possible."

"But if I can help," Frannie pleads with River. He shakes his head firmly.

"No, Fran. I don't want you involved. When you finally fall asleep at night, I'm awake and sitting in the chair watching for shadows with my gun locked and loaded and my knife hidden underneath the chair cushion. Ryley is the only one brave enough to mention what she's thinking, but the truth is, I've been thinking it too."

Evan stiffens beside me and I try to ease the tension in his arm to no avail.

"We need to check in with each other daily, no excuses," River says and the guys all agree.

"Ryley and I need to leave," Evan says abruptly and I know better to question his decision. I get up and hug Frannie, promising to call her in the morning and she says the same thing. We're going to follow what River says because we know it'll give him and Evan peace of mind. Plus, we'll leave a trace.

Evan grabs my hand and pulls me through the sand and into the parking lot. I have to jog to keep up and once we're in the car, I lock us in. He's speeds out of the parking lot, and heads toward home. After five minutes of silence I can't take it anymore.

"Talk to me, Archer." I use his last name to get a rise out of him. I've never really called him that except when we're fooling around. I know he likes it, but right now I just want his attention on me.

"I'm concerned, Ry. River and I... we were discussing this

earlier and the fact that you brought it up, means others are likely thinking the same thing. I don't like it."

I run my hand up and down his arm until he links his fingers with mine. "I don't either. I want to get home to EJ," I say, getting the reaction I'm looking for as Evan pushes down on the accelerator, breaking the speed limit.

The usual fifteen-minute drive takes us about eight. We're both out of the car and by each other's sides as quickly as we can be. When we get inside, relief washes over me as I find EJ snuggled up to my dad's side. Both of them are sound asleep. My dad is snoring so loudly I don't know how EJ is sleeping.

"Take EJ upstairs. I need to talk to your dad." I know better than to argue, and I carefully remove EJ from under my dad's arm. He grumbles, but wakes quickly and helps me lift EJ into my arms. I'm halfway upstairs when I hear the quiet whispers of Evan and my dad.

I could stay on the stairs and listen, but the truth of the matter is that I'm scared of what I brought up this evening. I wish I were the only one who felt this way. I'd feel more secure knowing it's just me being paranoid. But the fact that Frannie has been having these feelings scares me. Not to mention the fact that Penni and Claire seem to have disappeared and the way Rask's parents reacted.

If they're trying to scare us into compliance, it's working.

Whoever they are.

The next two things I hear are the front door shutting and the telltale sign of a gun being loaded. My SEAL is back.

TWENTY-EIGHT

Evan

AS SOON AS JENSEN'S in his car and driving down the street, I call for Deefur, step back into the house and lock the door. Blinds are pulled and windows checked. I open the closet door, pull out my black case and carry it to the couch. Ryley's upstairs putting EJ to bed and as soon as she's done I'll be doing a sweep of the house. Deefur follows me, keeping on my heels. I wish I hadn't missed the time he was growing up. I wanted to train him to protect Ryley. That's why I bought him. I wanted her to feel safe and never have to worry. It's in a dog's nature to protect his master, and I want to make sure he knows just how valuable her life is to me.

I look over my gun and make sure everything checks out before I load the bullets. I know Ryley can hear the gun when I move a bullet into the chamber. I'm okay with that as long as she knows she's safe. I told Jensen about our suspicions, and he's going to see if he can get Carole to back off a bit before anyone catches wind of what she's doing. The last thing I want is for her to be in the middle of a hot bed of issues that she can't escape. We need to find the pilot from the C-130 we traveled on and see if we can get him to talk. If we can, I think we'll start uncovering a lot.

Ryley comes down the stairs in a pair of yoga pants and a tank top. My eyes immediately fall onto her breasts, and I wish they hadn't. I swallow hard and set my gun down, hoping she'll grace me with her presence.

"Do you remember how to shoot?" I ask her, thinking back to the many hours we spent at the shooting range.

"I do," she says as she sits next to me. "My gun is upstairs. It's sitting on my bed."

I nod and kiss her briefly before getting up and taking the steps two at a time. She knows where I'm going and knows what to expect. Ryley knows I'm going to keep her and EJ safe. They'll have to shoot me in the head before they get to my family.

After I check her gun over, making sure it's loaded and ready, I click the safety on and set it in her beside drawer. I notice that there are two pictures on her table. One is of her, Nate and me. The other is of her and EJ. It gives me hope that she has either put the photos of Nate away or she never had any. It's the small things that are allowing me to look forward to the next day.

When I get back downstairs, Ryley is curled up and asleep on the couch. My options are limited, and I'll be damned if I'm going to carry her upstairs when I can sit next to her all night. I gently lay a blanket over her and watch her snuggle into the sofa. I could sit across from her – this view gives me excellent view of the front door – but I don't need it. I know we're being overly paranoid, but we all have too much at stake to not have our senses heightened and make sure we're prepared. I take the open space next to her, with my back to the wall. It's the best vantage point for me and if by chance something happens, I know Ryley can shoot a gun.

I slide my knife under the couch and settle in next to Ryley, picking up her feet to rest them in my lap and turn on the television. I'm far too wired to even think about sleep. In fact, it's the last thing I want to do. I really should go to the gym and take out my aggression on the bag, but I'm not leaving Ryley and EJ alone if I can help it. I'm going to have to talk to Ry about her daily schedule and find out when she's going back to work. Hell, I need to find out if I'm still being paid.

Flipping through the channels, I decide to watch the U.S.A. Summer basketball game. It's annoying to see these professional athletes getting all the attention when it should be the college kids. These guys make too much money for a lack of effort. At least when the college guys are playing, they're playing to make a difference, not a paycheck. I keep the volume low so I can hear the noises from outside. The house creaks, just as it does every night. Deefur lies at my feet, his ears perking with every noise. I like that. I like knowing that he's alert.

Ryley rolls over and looks at me. She's only been asleep for an hour and it's not even late. It's just emotionally and physically exhausting talking about the shit that's going on in our lives. I don't blame her for needing a catnap. I'd love to lie down next to her, but tonight's one of those nights where I'm going to stay awake just to see what's going on outside. I'm not expecting much, but that doesn't mean I'm letting my guard down.

The shit McCoy's going through scares me. His wife is gone and there's no trace of where she is. That shit is messed up and I can't even imagine what the hell he's feeling. Hell, I don't even know how he's functioning right now, but he is. I can tell you this, whoever is behind us being dead for six years better hope they take care of themselves because we'll be coming for them and it won't be pretty. McCoy is a torture specialist and the rest of us just might forget about ethics.

I startle when my cheek is slapped. I jump, causing EJ to laugh. I look at my watch and back at my son who is staring at me. He looks so much like I did when I was his age, but with Ryley's hair color. Ryley is still asleep next to me and the TV is showing some infomercial. I can't believe I fell asleep. My subconscious could be telling me that we're safe, but I'm not sure I'm buying it. I look at my watch and see that it's just after four a.m. and he shouldn't be awake right now.

I put my fingers to my lips, letting him know that he needs to be quiet. Quickly glancing at Ryley, I make sure she's still sleeping and pull EJ up onto the couch. I have to bite the inside of my cheek when he snuggles into my side. I've dreamed of moments like this with my wife on one side and my son on the other. The wife part I'm working on, but having my son in my arms is the most surreal feeling I've ever experienced.

Flipping the channel to a cartoon, I lean back and bring EJ closer to me. He sets his head on my chest, pulling his blanket closer. I had one when I was his age right up until I started school. I used to carry it everywhere. My dad hated it, but I didn't care. My blanket was my buddy and was the only one I could confide in.

I maneuver EJ as he haphazardly lies across my lap. This position allows me to run my fingers through his hair. I have so much to make up for and starting this morning, we're going to do some family things and maybe even Dad and EJ stuff. I'm not expecting an overnight adjustment, but I need to be in his life almost twenty-four seven because I'm his dad, regardless of how things have been the past few years.

The day Ryley told me she was pregnant I wanted to kick my own ass for not asking her to marry me the moment she told me she was ready to start a family. I'm such a pig-headed machismo that all I thought about was knocking her up. I never thought about how they wouldn't be taken care of if I were to die – which apparently I did – which also means that someone received my financial payout, and I have a feeling I know who did.

'I love you,' she says as her hand slips into mine. I turn my head, the grass we're laying in poking me in my ear and eye. She laughs and it's the most magical sound I've ever heard.

'I love you, Ryley.' Men don't understand the importance of telling their girls that they love them and not saying 'I love you, too'. Adding that extra word almost takes away from the meaning, like it's a reflex reaction. It's not the same, at least not for me. She needs to know that I love her as much, if not more and her saying it first doesn't diminish that for me.

Ryley rests her head on my shoulder and tickles me along my waistband. Her fingers brush along my boxers and in and out of the fine hairs on my stomach. It's a good thing my hands are behind my head or I'd be moving her hand over the top of my shorts.

'I'm pregnant, Evan.'

I don't have to ask her to repeat herself. I heard her loud and clear. I roll onto my side, taking her with me so I can look into her eyes.

'Tell me again,' I say because I so want to hear those words come off her sweet lips.

'I'm pregnant.' Her face lights up with so much magic, it's hard for me to contain my own smile. I move in quickly, bringing her lips to mine and rolling her on top of me.

'Are you happy?' I ask, thinking I already know her answer.

'I'm so happy, Evan. We're going to have a family.'

'Do you want a boy or girl?'

She laughs. 'I think a boy.'

I raise my eyebrow at her. 'Really? I thought you'd be all over having a little girl running around.'

'Not with you as her dad and Nate as her uncle. The poor girl would never be able to date. No, I think I want a happy, healthy boy who looks like his daddy so when you're not home I still have my Evan with me.'

'I'm just happy that you're pregnant, Ry. Our lives are almost complete.'

'You make me complete, Evan. I don't need a child to feel that way, I just need you.'

'God, I love you, Ryley. We should get married.'

She sits up partially and eyes me. 'I'm not marrying you, Evan Archer.'

I sit up, holding her to me. I love that her legs wrap around my waist. Placing one hand on her stomach and the other on her cheek, I kiss her softly. 'You're my life, Ryley. I want nothing more than to marry you, and we should've done it back when you turned eighteen. So, I'm asking you now. Ryley Clarke, will you do me the honor being my wife?'

'Yes... yes, I will.'

I jump and my skin begins to tingle when a loud thunking echoes outside the house. I shake Ryley with my fingers to my lips. She startles and looks around until she focuses on me. I motion for her to take EJ upstairs. I don't have to tell her what to do. She knows.

As soon as he's off my lap, I pull my gun out from under the couch and move toward the door. I keep the blinds closed and listen for footsteps. They're walking up the stairs and on the porch. The last thing I want to do is hurt someone with my son just upstairs, but those bastards have it coming.

The screen door opens; the small squeak is everyone's worst enemy. I turn the handle slowly and peak outside. Their back is to me and at my advantage.

"Who the fuck are you?" I say, with the barrel of my gun

pressing against their skull. "Turn around slowly or it's lights out."

Their hands go up slowly and they turn.

I drop my gun instantly. "What the fuck are you doing here?"

"Mom kicked me out when I sided with you. I need a place to stay."

I shake my head and pull Livvie into my arms. "I almost ended your life. You might want to try and call first."

She shrugs. "I would, but you don't have a cell phone and Ryley and I aren't exactly on speaking terms."

Picking up her luggage, I motion for her to go inside. "If you're staying here, you better fix shit with Ryley."

Livvie nods. "I will, I promise."

TWENTY-NINE

Ryley

MY BEDROOM LIGHT IS OFF, and I crack open the door so I can hear what's going on downstairs. I keep my hand over my mouth so I don't make a sound. EJ is sound asleep in my bed, spread out and taking up as much space as possible. My eyes close when I hear Evan's gun cock. I don't know who's outside, but I feel sorry for them. My father has always said never come between a man and his family because you'll never win.

Footsteps on the stairs and down the hall cause me to move away from the door. I stand, with my back facing EJ. My legs are spread at equal width and my arms are raised. The Glock is at my ready and aimed at my door.

"Ryley," Evan opens my door slowly, his hand coming in first before he pushes the door open. He stands in the doorway with his hands up, his gun in his waistband. "You can put your gun down." Tears fill my eyes as he moves closer. By the time he places his hand on the top of my gun. I'm shaking.

"Come on, babe, lower your gun." He pushes it down gently. "I know you're scared and I am too, but I can guarantee you no one will ever hurt you or EJ."

"Wh—what's going on?"

Evan takes the gun from my hand and disarms it, setting it back in my drawer. "Livvie is downstairs. My mom kicked her out and she needs a place to stay. She said she would've called, but I don't have a phone and you guys aren't friendly."

I sit on the edge of my bed and clutch at my legs. "I don't like this, Evan. I don't want to panic every time someone comes knocking on the door."

Evan sits down next to me and wraps his arm around me. "This is my fault; I got you worked up. Everything you said earlier just got to me. I don't like what has happened to us, and I hate that I have no control over it."

I lean into Evan and try to relax. My body feels heavy and it's so odd to think of how fast your adrenaline starts to pump when fear sets in. I don't know what I was afraid of. I know Evan isn't going to let anything happen to us. But the thought that someone might be in our home and a danger to us really gets to me.

"Why don't you try and get some sleep? I'm going to go back downstairs and sit with Livvie." I peer up at Evan, who meets my gaze immediately. I see it. I see it all in his eyes. The love he has for EJ, me and us. I initiate the kiss even though I shouldn't. I know I'm going to hell and that karma is going to come back to bite me in the ass, but I need to feel him against me even if it's just his lips.

He kisses me back, slowly. His lips are soft as they move against mine. "You're my life," Evan whispers against my mouth, and I know this is true. I know we can be together if I just allow it.

Nate…

He needs to come home. He and Evan need to sit down and figure this out. We need to be a family and figure out why this is happening to us.

"I used to think I had a pretty amazing life. From the

outside I had everything others wanted. I had a wonderful family, and I still do. I had a committed boyfriend who I had a future with. I was doing well in college and on my way to having a career that I could move around when my boyfriend needed to move. Then one day, the rug gets pulled out from under me, and I'm flat on my ass. My family is still wonderful, but they're walking on eggshells around me. My committed boyfriend, who promised to come home, did, but in a wooden box all the while leaving me with the best gift possible, our son."

"Where are you going with this Ryley?"

I shake my head, not sure where this is heading. "I don't know, Evan. Tonight, everything just seems…" I stand and start pacing to get the blood flowing again. "I love your brother and I know you don't want to hear me say those words, but I do. I always have. But not like I love you. The love I have for you is all consuming. Every fiber of my being tingles when I'm near you, and that's something I can't deny.

"The day we met, I thought you were my knight in shining armor even though I didn't need saving. Being the new girl at school was something I was used to. What I wasn't used to was you and all the feelings you were bringing out in me so quickly. That first night, I tried to call you. I couldn't bring myself to dial the last number. I fell asleep with my stupid pink phone in my hand and anxiety in my heart because I felt my one shot at true love slipping away.

"I guess what I'm saying, Evan, is that I'm not going to marry Nate." My eyes focus on his, as his smile grows wide. I shake my head. "I'm not going to marry you either."

"What?" he chokes out as his face reddens.

"We're not ready. We've been apart for six years and I've changed. You need to know who I am now, and not live in the past. You need time to get to know your son and be a presence in his life. Nate isn't going to go away and you need to accept that and accept that he and EJ have a relationship. I'm not going to take that away from EJ."

"I'd never ask that of EJ, or of you. It pains me to say that, Ryley." He stands and takes the few steps to where I'm standing. He pulls my arms around his waist and places his hands on the side of my face. His hands are soft and warm. "I've waited a god-damn long time to be with you again and if I have to wait a little bit more, so be it. As long as you want to be with me, I'll be here waiting."

"Will you move back home?" I ask, abruptly. "I want you here. You need to be here with EJ and be a part of our routine."

"This is where I want to be, Ry. Everything I need is here in this house. I promise not to pressure you into anything. I'll be patient and wait even though I'm nursing the mother of all blue balls cases. I really think they're about to explode."

He's so dramatic, but he makes me laugh. I can't contain my laughter and end up snorting. "Oh god," I say, covering my mouth and nose. "I can't believe I just did that."

"Just face it. I bring out the best in you."

Nodding. "You do, and I love you for it."

Evan leans down and kisses me briefly. "I think I need to stop doing that if I'm going to be a good boy."

A good boy? I'm not sure Evan Archer has even been considered a good boy since he turned five. "I don't mind a few kisses here and there, but what happened in the car yesterday can't happen again."

"But... that was so fun," he whines. I shake my head and step away from him. EJ is still sprawled out on my bed, but his eyes are open. I lay down next him and snuggle into his neck.

"No, momma," he whines just like his dad. EJ rubs his face and pretends to go back to sleep but his eyes are blinking so fast I know he's awake.

The bed dips and Evan slides next to EJ. Evan rests on his elbow and stares from EJ to me, back and forth.

"He's so beautiful, Ryley. Someone is going to pay for what they've done to us," he says quietly.

"I know, Evan. I want them to as well."

Evan reaches for my hand, pulling me close to EJ while he brings my hand to his chest, tucking it under his arm. We cocoon EJ and this is one of those moments that I've waited for, for a very long time.

THIRTY

Evan

SUNLIGHT STREAMS THROUGH THE window. I shift without opening my eyes. My hand feels warm and tight. For the first time in a long time, I'm waking up in a bed next to the love of my life. The bonus is that our son is in between us. My eyes open slowly, so the sun won't blind me. I wonder why Ryley left her curtain open. So many thoughts run through my mind about the security of the house, about her and EJ. They're my priority. I will protect them at all cost.

The first sight my eyes behold, glowing in the morning light is Ryley. She looks at peace. There are no worry lines marring her face, no anger or disappointment in her eyes. No, those emotions will appear later. We can't make it through a day without those two emotions bringing us down.

My eyes fall onto my son, who has rolled closer to me. My heart dances a little jig, thinking this is a victory, but I know it will be short lived. He's only this close because gravity has made the space next to me available to him. As much as I want him to recognize me as his dad, I can't push him. Doing so would backfire and likely drive him away, unless Nate helps. But that scenario is highly unlikely.

I'm not sure what to expect when I see him. Will he be

shocked that I'm here? Angry? Disappointed? The reunions that we've had in the past will not be what this one will be. I want to act like we're eight again and wrestle him to the ground for the last Twinkie. Except this time we'll be fighting for Ryley, although I sort have already won. However, I'm not stupid enough to take her not marrying him for granted. I'm going to have to work my ass off. Six years is too long to be without someone and she moved on, like I'd expect her to.

I didn't.

I couldn't.

Everything that she and I had built from our teens has to start over. The only benefit is that I can woo her properly without asking my parents to borrow a car or a few dollars for ice cream.

Ice cream... that is what we need today. My little family needs to be pampered and shown just how much I love them. A trip to the zoo, some ice cream and a walk along the beach with Deefur is what the doctor ordered. Or she would if I told Doc Howard about my plan. I think she'd agree.

Gazing back down at my family, it's a shame to wake them, but I want to utilize every moment possible. I have this feeling in the pit of my stomach that our world is about to be rocked again and I can't shake it. Whatever it is, whatever's coming, I'll be prepared.

I gently move a few strands of hair from Ryley's face. She startles, but relaxes the moment my fingertips trail down the side of her face. She was made for me and I've often thought how my life would be drastically different had I not hit her with the football that day. Or if her mom didn't get reassigned to Bremerton. Those thoughts make me feel empty and hollow. I can honestly say that I wouldn't be the man I am today without Ryley in my life.

"You look deep in thought," her voice brings me back to the here and now. Seeing her like this, no words can describe how sexy I think she is.

"I was just thinking about how I'm a much better man because of you."

Ryley rolls her eyes. She doesn't believe me and that's okay. It's hard for people to take such a meaningful compliment.

"Hey, I thought we'd go to the zoo, get some ice cream and take Deefur to the beach?" I make it sound like it's not my plan. Like I don't need to do this today.

"Did you just 'hey' me?"

I look at her questioningly and her eyebrow rises. "Um, yeah I guess." I shrug, not realizing or even remembering what I said to her. I'm too lost in thoughts of holding her hand while we walk barefoot down the beach with our son and dog a few steps ahead of us.

"Are you okay?" she asks because she can read me like a book. I nod, although it's not very reassuring.

"Momma, I'm starving."

EJ speaks, but doesn't open his eyes. This is the second time I've seen him do this. I make a mental note to ask Ryley about it later.

"Aunt Livvie is downstairs," she whispers in his ear. He bolts right up and rubs his eyes before maneuvering himself off the bed. I completely forgot about Livvie showing up in the early morning hours. Then I fell asleep up here, leaving her downstairs.

"Shit, Ry. I forgot Livvie was here." I cover my face and groan. I love my sister and I've missed her, but I'm not sure her moving in here with Ryley is an option. She and I are trying to rebuild what we had, and I'm trying to forge a relationship with my son. The last thing I want is for Ryley to feel crowded or EJ to ignore me in favor of my sister. As much as this is my house, I can't assume it's going to be okay for Livvie to stay here. Not to mention, Nate technically lives here too.

"I'm going to go take a shower. I'll meet you downstairs."

Everything about her telling me she's going to take a shower seems so real. I watch as she rolls off the bed and into the bathroom. Once the door closes, I stare up at the ceiling and think how natural being here is, yet not forgetting that once Nate returns, shit's going to escalate quickly. He's been in love with Ryley since high school. He's not going to let her go easily. I like to think I have the advantage.

As much as I want to lie in bed all day I need to be proactive. I have to try and establish a bond with my son before Nate comes home. I never thought I'd have to fight for my family, but I do and I will.

I shower quickly in the guest bathroom, which is technically mine and EJ's and head downstairs. Ryley and Livvie are sitting at the kitchen island drinking coffee. It warms me thinking they're trying to fix things between them.

"What's on your arms?"

EJ is sitting on the couch, his little legs bouncing up and down. He's ready to go and have fun today. I look down at my arms, moving them around so he can see what I have.

"They're called tattoos."

"Can I get one?"

I laugh remembering how angry my mom was when I came home from basic training with one on my arm. I think this is one of those parental moments that I have to craft my answer carefully. If I tell him no, he'll remember and do it anyway. Chances are he'll get it done in some seedy shop by some half-assed artist. I tell him yes, and he wants to go get one now and somehow I don't think Ryley would be in favor of that.

Sitting down, I take a chance and pull him onto my lap. He doesn't fight me, and there's a little pang of hope coursing through my body reminding me that I need to create and steal as many of these moments with him that I can.

"I bet you that we can find the special kind of little kid

tattoos that your mom will allow you to have. When I got my first one, your grandma was so mad at me."

"She was?" he looks shocked when I bring up my mom.

I nod, unable to keep the big ass grin from taking over my face. "She was so angry she threw a pillow at me."

His little mouth drops open. "Did it hurt?"

"Nah. Don't tell grandma this, but she throws like a baby."

EJ starts to giggle and it's the most amazing sound I've ever heard. I quickly follow suit and wish I had a camera to capture this moment.

"Do you want to frow the ball wif me?"

I stop laughing and stare at my son. He'll never know the magnitude of his question. "I'd love to, EJ. What kind are we throwing?"

He shrugs. "I hab football, baseball and baketball."

I fight the urge to rejoice and pull him into my arms. I don't want to scare him so I just nod and feel the immediate loss of him when he climbs off my lap.

"Come on, Eban."

Boy, doesn't he know I'd follow him anywhere for these little bits of time? I stand and quickly follow him outside. When I pass Ryley she's smiling, and I can't resist the urge to kiss her. So I do.

"I love you. Thank you for him," I whisper into her before heading out back to throw the ball around with my son.

THIRTY-ONE

Ryley

"WHAT ARE YOU GOING to do?" Livvie asks. I shake my head before bringing my cup of coffee to my lips. I'm watching Evan and EJ toss the ball around in the back yard. Evan is helping him work on his stance, showing him the proper technique. To his credit, Nate has kept EJ active in sports. Whether they're watching games on TV, attending events or playing in the backyard, Nate's kept EJ interested. Aside from the military, sports are something the twins shared.

Earlier this morning, lying with Evan and having EJ in the middle was another image I could only project in my mind previously. Watching them outside, bonding like this, is another. It's like someone plucked all my wishes from the past six years out of my mind and transformed them into real-life.

I'm not dumb enough to think my bubble isn't going to burst... explode. It's going to happen and there isn't anything that anyone can do about it. People are going to get hurt. It's already started with Julianne kicking Livvie out. I know Julianne is hurting and confused, we all are. But where she should be embracing the fact that her son is home, she's not.

Maybe she's like Rask's parents, unable to believe that the military could do something like this. I don't want to believe that either, but there's no other explanation.

If I were the only one affected I might have a hard time understanding where he's been, but I'm not. His unit has been dead for years only to show up as if nothing happened. As much as it pains me to say this, I almost wish he were a POW because then we'd have closure. We'd have the answers we need to move on. Right now, all we have are assumptions and fear. Fear that if we ask too many questions, something's going to happen to us.

"I don't know," I say, honestly. I don't know what to do. I know I want to try with Evan, but also know it's not fair to Nate. "What do you think if I ask the twins to not reenlist and we'll move to some isolated farm land where I can have multiple husbands?"

Livvie laughs, not because it's funny, but because of the absurdity of what I just said. Neither man would even come close to agreeing. Both are possessive in their own ways.

"I can't believe how much EJ is like Evan," she says now standing next to me. "I never saw it before because Ev wasn't here, but now I do."

"God, everything is going to be so complicated when Nate gets home. Why would people do this to us... to anyone for that matter?"

Livvie puts her hand on my shoulder. This is the first time we've been able to stay civil in a long time. Maybe it was her love for Evan that drove a wedge between us when Nate and I started dating. She's always been closer to Evan.

"People are evil. People don't stop and think about who they're hurting. They have a goal in mind or they're trying to cover up something and will stop at nothing to succeed. As long as they're protected, what do they care if they're hurting families? What do they care if they're destroying hopes and dreams? They don't. They only care about themselves."

I push away a tear and tell her she's right. Livvie steps away when she sees EJ and Evan bounding up the stairs. I move over to the sink to rinse out my mug and wait for the room to start spinning and for my skin to start tingling. I know the moment he's stepped into the room, and I close my eyes and bask in way I'm feeling. His hands rest on my hips and he leans forward pressing into my backside. I inhale deeply, taking in his fresh scent and cologne.

"How do you feel about taking EJ and Deefur down to the beach? Let them run around for a bit?"

I nod, liking the idea. Evan doesn't give me a chance to turn around before he's moved away from me. I can hear him faintly talking to his sister in the other room. EJ is upstairs hollering about something, and I find myself laughing. Laughing at the fact that my house is noisy. That two of the people that I love most in life are bonding and forging a relationship. I'm laughing because I feel like I'm in a fairytale romance with a murder-mystery twist. The sad part is I don't know the ending.

When Evan and I bought this house, we chose the prime location. While the beach isn't in my backyard, it is within walking distance. EJ carries his bag of sand castle toys while I carry the beach towels. Evan has a cooler perched on his shoulder, and Deefur is walking two steps ahead of EJ with his leash dragging on the sidewalk.

Once we hit the sand, I slip off my shoes and hurry to catch up with my boys. Evan finds us a spot where EJ can play safely in the sand without him covering us with water from his sand castle building operation. I love that it's not overly hot today, but am weary of the dark cloud that looms on the horizon.

"Do you see that cloud?"

Evan nods. "I'll watch it. If it starts moving fast, we'll head home." He picks up Deefur's tennis ball and tosses it toward the water. The dog takes off, jumping over the waves and going under until he surfaces with it in his mouth. Evan throws it again before sitting down next to me.

"This is nice."

"Yeah, it is. I just hate that I've missed so much." He slips off his shirt and I gasp. It's been so long since I've seen him like this. I do the only levelheaded thing there is to do. I pull out my bottle of sunscreen and move behind him.

He hisses when the cool lotion touches his back. "That shit's cold, babe."

"I know, but you need it. You'll burn, and I'm not going to listen to you whine."

"I don't whine," he says, earning an eye roll from me. I take this opportunity to massage his shoulder muscles and his back. "God, I've missed this."

"Yeah, look at me already giving you a massage."

He turns his head and peers at me sideways. "You love touching me. You're using it as an excuse to touch my body. Oh my god, woman, you're using me."

I pinch his side, causing him to laugh.

"Do I get to rub you down?"

"I'd say yes if I didn't think you were trying to cop a feel."

Evan places his hand over his heart and falls over. He's so dramatic. "I can't believe you would say such a thing about me."

I roll my eyes at him in mock disgrace. Putting the sunblock back, I stand and take off my shirt and wriggle out of my cut-offs. I feel his eyes on me, but I don't make contact. I don't want to lose my nerve as I walk away from him.

"Hey, Ry?" he yells after I've taken a few steps away from him. I look at him over my shoulder and find him in the same position that I left him. Except I'm certain his tongue is hanging out. "Why don't you come back here and sit on my lap?"

I shake my head and continue to walk toward EJ, who is frantically digging in the sand. Deefur is laying next him, not caring that he's being buried alive.

"Do you need some help?" I ask, kneeling down.

"You can do the digging." He hands me his shovel and starts filling his buckets full of sand. I continue to work on his moat making sure to place my sand on the outside, away from where he's building. I ignore the dark shadow that belongs to Evan who's standing next to me. I purposely start to bury his feet.

"EJ, who taught you how to build a sand castle?"

"Papa," he says without looking at Evan.

"Did papa tell you that you need prisoners?"

EJ and I both look at Evan, both of us confused. "I dunno." EJ shrugs and goes back to packing his bucket.

"You should run, Ryley."

"Excuse me?"

"Hey, EJ. I need your help, little man. On the count of three I'm going to pick up your mom and throw her into the ocean. In about two seconds she's going to start running so I need you to help me catch her."

He's right. I takes me about two seconds to realize what's about to happen before I get up and start running. I chance a look over my shoulder, and he's still standing there. I know I'm doomed. He's a SEAL. This is his playground.

EJ and Evan start after me, and I'm screaming. Deefur is also chasing me, and the little shit is cutting me off, driving me back toward Evan.

"Get her, Eban."

"You're supposed to help me, EJ!" I yell just as two very strong arms wrap around my waist.

"Such a little tease running around in your bikini." Evan lifts me up and throws me over his shoulder like I weigh nothing. My lovely son is behind us, cheering him on. I shake my fist at EJ, only to earn more laughter.

I close my eyes when I hear water splashing. It's going to be cold, but I have to show no weakness. Evan has taught me better. The second I'm lifted off his shoulder, I'm squeezing my eyes shut and closing my mouth. Evan makes good on his threat as I'm suddenly under water.

When I surface, EJ is on Evan's hip and Deefur is standing next to him. They're smiling. This is the family I've always dreamed about.

THIRTY-TWO

Nate

_____

COMING HOME TO AN empty house is not my idea of happiness. I've been counting the hours until I could return home. Until I could hold Ryley and play ball with EJ in the backyard. This mission was short compared to some, and longer than I wanted to be gone. I have no control over the time though. I'm just happy to be home.

The house has an eerie feel, almost somber. It's too quiet for my liking. I turn on the TV to create some background noise. The luggage in the corner catches my eye. I rifle through it. I'm nosey. It's my nature. It's all women's clothing but nothing Ryley would wear. Maybe Carter and Lois had a fight while I was gone and she's been staying here. I doubt it, but it's better than thinking Ryley has suddenly taken on a transient with her fashion taste.

I walk into the kitchen and pull a beer out of the fridge. I should call Ryley and tell her I'm home, but surprising her would be best, I think. I love seeing the look on her face when I come home. The way she feels pressed against my body after I've been gone. I've missed her terribly and need to hold her.

Sitting down on the couch, I pick up the pad of paper,

hoping to find a note as to where she might be. It's just her doodles, the silly little drawings that she used to do back in high school.

She draws swirly designs all over her notepad. I don't know why girls do this. Is it so they don't have to make eye contact with us? If so, that's the stupidest reason ever. She didn't even move when I sat down. I saw her in the hall earlier and almost lost my shit. Evan is going to freak out when he finds out. I send him a quick text, letting him know that the angel that saved him from purgatory is sitting next to me in class. I sort of want to ask her to look at me so I can razz him later about the shiner he gave her. I've never seen him so pussy whipped by a girl he doesn't even know.

I wish I could remember her name. If I did, I could introduce myself again. I wasn't paying attention yesterday because I thought she was just another piece of ass for Evan. But he acted differently around her at the park, and I've never seen him stare at the phone for so long. That's where I found him this morning – asleep with his head on top of the phone. He had a nice indent when he woke up.

She peers at me, and I smile. She probably thinks I'm creepy. I probably am creepy. Her head pops up and now she's full on staring. I close my mouth, afraid that I have something in my teeth. Evan has been making me drink those damn protein shakes in the morning to bulk up, but I know I brushed my teeth. There can't be any residue left. Right?

'You look just like your brother,' she blurts out and I'm rewarded with the most glorious shade of red as she blushes. Her beautiful hair, I'd say it was the color of a red autumn leaves, tries to hide her face, and I'm tempted to reach out and push it behind her ear.

Wait, what?

This is Evan's girl.

I can't touch her.

But I want to.

I laugh, and it's awkward. She turns to face me again. Her eyes pierce mine. She thinks I'm laughing at her. I'm not. I'm laughing at my idiotic heart that is falling for a girl my brother desperately wants. Oh, the irony.

'We're twins, and you just made the other me very happy.' Where do I come up with this crap? We're twins? And why do I care if he's happy? I want her for myself. Maybe she'll see just how much of a douche Evan can be, and I can console her.

She clears her throat and faces the front. I want her to turn and stare at me so I can form the perfect picture tonight before going to bed. I want to memorize every inch of her porcelain face and hold her delicate hands in mine. I want to protect her from the world.

I turn away when she glances at me. I shouldn't have these feelings but I can't help it. Evan's right, she's an angel. But if she's the angel, he most certainly is the devil and I know I'll have to bide my time until he's moved on. I'll be there to mend her broken heart, even if the wait kills me.

Evan texts back asking me if I'm serious. I could lie, but that will only work until he sees her himself. She's new; everyone will be talking about her. I can't hide her as much as I'd love to.

'Evan has been pacing by the phone waiting for you to call. He's going to be outside that door when the bell rings now that he knows you're here.'

She looks at the door and back at me. Her expression is stoic. Her hands clutch the end of her desk, and her knuckles turn white.

'What was your name again?' I ask my tongue thick in my throat.

'Ryley Clarke,' her voice is barely above a whisper but it's enough to make the hairs on my arm stand tall.

'What's yours?'

I like that she cares even if she's just returning the gesture.

'Nate. Nate Archer.' This is my opportunity to touch her so I extend my hand for her to shake. I feel my eyes go wide when we shake hands. 'Like I said, Evan will be very happy to see you.' I want to add that she should run in the opposite direction and that I'll be there to meet her. I'm the good one of the bunch. Not him.

My heart races the closer the second hand gets to the bell. I wish

I had never sent that text and just talked to her myself. What harm would that have done? I could've easily told Evan I forgot what she looked like. He wouldn't have bought it since he spent the night reciting everything that he loved about her. I know once he gets her into the backseat of his car he'll be done with her. I won't mind. I can't fight what my heart wants.

The bell signals the end of class and Mr. Reed throws his pen onto his desk and waves the students out. It's only the first day and he already looks flustered. I gather my things slowly and walk down the aisle staying one step behind Ryley. I'm trying not to watch her, but I can't help it.

I let her go in front of me and as soon as we're both facing the door, I see Evan. His head is bent slightly and he's watching her like a hawk watches his prey. When Donna, his weekly 'friend' walks by, I think he'll start watching her, but her presence doesn't faze him. That doesn't bode well for me.

I hate my brother right now. The coolness oozes off him. I didn't get the sex appeal gene. I got the brains. Why can't I have both? He beckons her with his finger and she goes, just like every other girl in this school. He looks up at and catches me watching and shakes his head. He's telling me she's off limits.

I don't wait to see what happens next. I put my head down and walk to my locker. Letting the regret build with each step I take.

I should've never texted him.

Footsteps bound up the front porch steps. I place my beer on the table and smile at the memory of the first day I met Ryley. Everything could've been different. But like I predicted, I was here to pick up the pieces when Evan died. It's not how I wanted things to be with us, but I'll take whatever I can get.

The front door opens and Ryley walks in. She's laughing and looking behind her. She doesn't know I'm here, reminding me that we need to talk about security and her being cautious when I'm not home. I see the top of EJ's head, knowing instantly that someone is carrying him. He's being held too high up and I know that it can't be Lois holding him.

They step in and all eyes are on me. My throat closes as we stand there, staring at each other. I blink, closing my eyes tightly and pray that when I open them all I see are Ryley and EJ standing before me.

When I open them my worst nightmare has come true. A ghost is holding my son. The boy I've raised from the day he was born. A man I buried years ago stands before me, who just a moment ago was laughing with my fiancée.

I look from him to Ryley and back. I don't even want to think about what's been going on or how the hell he ended up in our living room.

"Daddy," EJ says, and the only solace I feel right now is running toward me after being set down. I scoop him up and look at my dead brother as he eyes me with his newly found possession.

"How are you here?" I ask, clearly in shock.

"Ah, don't be so surprised little brother. It's not like you didn't know I was alive."

I didn't.

Acknowledgments

To the girls that never let me down: Yvette, Emily, Georgette and Fallon. I know this story was difficult, but you listened to my vision and helped me execute it. And thank you Jennifer Wolfel for being my last set of eyes.

Carey Heywood & LP Dover: Thank you for taking this first draft and loving it even though it was a train wreck. The conversations we've had only made this story so much stronger.

Sarah Hansen: thank you for hearing my vision so many months ago and having not only the perfect image for Here with Me, but having the image ready for Choose Me.

Bloggers: This is such a general term and encompasses so many. If you were a part of the blog tour, thank you for taking a chance on me. If you tweeted, shared or commented on the Here with Me cover reveal, I thank you. The anticipation that has been shown means so much.

Art Liberty: You came into my life when I needed it the most. The guiding hand and vote of confidence means more to me than I'll ever be able to repay. I appreciate everything you've done for this story, and thank you for the beauty that is your daughter, Becca. Without her, I'd still be in a panic.

The Beaumont Daily: I really couldn't ask for a better street team or water tower gang – whatever you guys want to be called. You're an amazing group and so fun to be a part of.

Finally to my family: thank you for allowing me to play with my imagination.

About the Author

Heidi is a New York Times and USA Today Bestselling author.

Originally from the Pacific Northwest, she now lives in picturesque Vermont, with her husband and two daughters. Also renting space in their home is an over-hyper Beagle/Jack Russell, Buttercup and a Highland West/Mini Schnauzer, JiLL and her brother, Racicot.

When she's isn't writing one of the many stories planned for release, you'll find her sitting court-side during either daughter's basketball games.

Forever My Girl, is set to release in theaters on October 27, 2017, starring Alex Roe and Jessica Rothe.

Connect with Me!

www.heidimclaughlin.com
heidi@heidimclaughlin.com

Also by Heidi McLaughlin

Blind Reality

Twisted Reality

SOCIETY X

Dark Room

Viewing Room

Play Room

STANDALONE NOVELS

Stripped Bare

Blow

Sexcation

Made in the USA
Columbia, SC
02 November 2020

23873824R00120